Charles Schofield

Sketch Book

Prose and Poetry

Charles Schofield

Sketch Book
Prose and Poetry

ISBN/EAN: 9783337369880

Printed in Europe, USA, Canada, Australia, Japan

Cover: Foto ©Andreas Hilbeck / pixelio.de

More available books at **www.hansebooks.com**

SKETCH BOOK.

PROSE

AND

POETRY.

———

BY

CHARLES SCHOFIELD.

———

PRINTED FOR THE AUTHOR.
THE SAN FRANCISCO NEWS COMPANY.
1886.

INTRODUCTION.

THE following named pieces of prose and poetry, which compose the contents of this little book, were written at intervals of leisure during the last six years, while engaged prospecting quartz in the mountains of Tuolumne County, California, and they are very respectfully dedicated to an appreciative and generous public, by the Author.

CONTENTS.

MY EARLY YEARS AT HOME.

I WAS born and raised in a log cabin in the wild woods of central New York. My father having to clear up the heavily timbered land upon which we lived, with a large family to support (seven boys and five girls), and in very straitened circumstances, it may well be imagined that we all had to work very hard from the time that we were large enough to do anything, in order to make both ends of the year meet. Very little time was allowed for play or for instruction at the little country school house, which was located across the fields and through the woods, about one mile and a half from our residence.

While we were yet quite small we attended school pretty regularly during the pleasant summer months, only remaining home rainy days or when we were indisposed; but when older and able to do a little work, we only went to school a portion of the winter, when work was slack, and the snow not so deep as to make it impossible for us to force our way through it. At such times, we nearly always had books at home, from the school libraries (which had then been very recently established throughout the country), with which we spent nearly every idle hour, and by this means gained much useful knowledge.

Speaking of myself, individually, my mind was so much absorbed in reading histories and the lives of great men, of all nations and ages, that reading soon became a passion with me and often kept me up into the late hours of the night, by firelight when other lights were not to be had; and the next day I would think over what I had read, and would often repeat the whole story to my brothers, or other associates, in my own language while at work.

As time rolled on, I began to have a great longing for a more thorough and extensive education than my father had been able to give me at home. I laid the matter before him as well as I was able, and asked his permission to go away from home to school. To this proposition he would not listen for a moment. He said that I had as much schooling as any of my brothers, and all that he could afford to give me; that my work was needed on the farm, and that I must stay at home and work till I was twenty-one, as my older brothers had done before me. I told him that I did not expect him to be at the expense of sending me to school; but that I was able and willing to work and pay my own way, and would not put him to one dollar's expense. He would not listen to my plea, but told me, in the most emphatic terms, that there was no alternative for me but to remain upon the farm until I was of age. My father was a stern, resolute man, and it was not often that his children, or other persons about him, went contrary to his known wishes; but I could not endure the thought of being forever deprived of the bright and glorious fruit to be gathered from the tree of knowledge.

The outlook was a dreary one indeed; but having fell heir to a reasonable share of my father's temper and resolution, I finally determined to make a desperate effort to break the chains that bound me to home and kindred, and wander singly and alone through the wide world, in search of fame and fortune. But not having a dollar in the world, or scarcely a decent suit of clothes to wear, I found it no easy matter to make a start. Yet by far the hardest stroke of fortune that befell me then, or in any subsequent period of life, was the death of my kind and gentle mother. She who had always cheered and consoled me in all my troubles, had suddenly left us forever; she was truly an angel upon earth, and now an angel in Heaven. Her pure and spotless life and character have ever had a saving influence over the lives and destinies of all her children.

My two older brothers had become of age and left home; two sisters had also married and gone; and, although my favorite sister, next older than myself, remained at home and kept house for father, the old house no longer seemed like home to me. I continually longed to be away from home and at school. After having repeated interviews with my father upon the subject, all of which availed me nothing, my mind was at length wrought up to such a pitch that I determined to go at all events, whether he gave his consent or no. But being entirely without means to travel any distance, and very little acquainted with the world generally, I went to a neighboring farmer and engaged to work for him six months during the summer and fall for the usual wages. But at the end of my term of service, my father made demand for my wages and collected all of them, not even leaving me enough to purchase a suit of clothes for the winter.

But with all these sad discouragements, I did not give up the long cherished idea of commencing a regular course of schooling that winter. I went to a merchant in the nearest village, and, overcoming my embarrassment as well as I could, I freely told him of my necessities, my hopes, and desires, and finally asked him if he would sell me enough cloth to make me a good suit of winter clothing, on six months' credit, and also telling him at the same time, in what way I expected to raise the money. To this proposition he readily assented, and having obtained the desired cloth and trimmings, I went to the house of a married sister to have the clothes made up. Then finding a place near the village where I could do chores nights and mornings to pay for my board,

I attended a select school during all the long winter months, and made excellent progress with my studies.

The next spring, having borrowed a few dollars of a brother-in-law, and without letting my father know my destination, I left my native town of Marathon, Cortland County, New York, and traveled on foot across the country to Steuben County, about eighty miles distant, where my eldest brother was engaged in the business of lumbering, and rafting down the Conisteo, Shemung, and Susquebanna Rivers. Here I readily found employment at good wages during the rafting season, making three full trips down the above named rivers, and was home again, in Marathon, on the first day of June, with more than money enough to settle all my obligations, which I did with the greatest of pleasure. After making my friends at home a short visit, I again left for parts unknown, for the purpose of working at haying and harvesting, and earning money enough to enable me to commence at Homer Academy the first of the fall term. This time I went to Seneca County, New York, and after working hard nearly three months, was home again on the first of September, with money enough to set me all right for the fall and winter terms.

The next spring and summer I again sought the river and harvest fields in order to win more money, in which I was again successful; and then again returned to school as before. I kept up this routine with very little variation, with the exception of two winters, in which I taught school in western New York and Pennsylvania, as long as I attended school at the academy, or about five years, during which time I met with many interesting adventures, both upon water and in the field, some of which may be well worth relating.

RAFTING.

Being of stalwart frame, and lively turn of mind, I soon became quite an expert in river navigation,

and could handle a steering oar and navigate a raft
as well as the best of the old river-men; consequently,
after the first two or three trips, I always received extra wages, and usually remained down the river and
"steered through to tide" each spring as long as the
water held up high enough, or while there was anything to do, and usually received from three to seven
dollars per day, while the business lasted.

In rafting (out of the upper branches of the Susquehanna), each raft (and sometimes only part of a
raft) was run separate, on account of the short turns
in these small rivers; the pilot always handling the
forward oar, and the steersman the oar at the stern
of the raft, each having three or four extra men to
help push the oar through when dipped; but when
the main body of the great Susquehanna is reached,
several rafts are usually coupled together, and one
pilot and one steersman answer for the whole fleet;
but when the lower end of the great river is reached,
the rafts are separated and run singly among the
rocks, and through the wild, whirling rapids near its
mouth, and before we reach tide-water. And here,
too, for the last twenty-five or thirty miles, a new set
of pilots, steersmen, and extra hands are usually required to handle a raft with safety. All hands too
have to be wide-awake and lively, or the raft may go
crashing among the rocks on either side, and be torn
to pieces by strong currents and whirling eddies. As
tide pilots generally bargain to take the lumber
through these wild rapids at their own risk, for a
certain price, they are very careful in the selection of
a steersman, and the management of a raft generally
is intrusted more or less to his energy and skill.

These rafts being built beforehand, and ready for
a start, usually left the upper branches of the river
about the same time, or whenever the water was
high enough to float them down clear of all obstruc-
tions; and there was often much rivalry among up-
river pilots as to who should be first at Marietta, a

small town on the lower Susquehanna, where the rafts were usually turned over to tide pilots.

A RACE.

At one time my brother James, who was an up-river pilot, made a bet with Nelson Wetherby (who was generally acknowledged to be one of the best pilots on the river), of an oyster supper for all hands, that he would be first at Marietta that trip. Both left Addison, Steuben County, New York, the same day, with two rafts each, and Wetherby a little ahead. I steered that trip for my brother. We had good luck in getting out of the Conisteo River into the Shemung, and got our two rafts coupled together, discharging the extra pilot, but did not see anything of Wetherby till long after we had got upon the broad bosom of the great Susquehanna, although we had run all one night in order to overtake and pass him. But on reaching Northumberland, one day just before dark, we found him safely moored to the shore, just above the great Shamokin dam. We hailed him, but passed on, hoping to get safely through the shute before dark, and then make another night's run. But it had already begun to be quite dark before we reached the dam, and not being able to see clearly, we ran onto the wing dam of the shute with the forward end of the raft, and the hind end immediately swung round to the shore, closing up the entrance to the shute, the strong current bending the two rafts in the form of a crescent, but the good Norway couplings held, or we would have gone pell-mell through the shute (which was only wide enough for two rafts abreast) with the speed of a race horse, which must have proved our certain destruction. But seeing that the rafts had come to a stand, and stood the shock without breaking, we cooked and ate our supper, and then went fearlessly to bed in our little cabin in the center of our rafts; but if anything heavy had struck us during the night, and forced us double through the shute, none would have been left to tell the story of our end.

The next morning, after cooking and eating break-fast, we fastened the hind end of our rafts to some posts on shore, with strong cables, and then fixing some temporary ones, we cut the couplings near the center, so that each half swung round by itself, and the forward half slid from the wall and went through the shute, with men enough to manage and land it below. We soon had the other half through the shute and landed at the same place; but while we were putting the raft into running order again, Mr. Weatherby came past and bid us good-morning; but we were soon under way, and followed him close all that day and again passed him just before night, safely landed just above Green's dam. We passed on and made the shute safely, and the next day were safely moored at Marietta, having won our bet, and beat the boss pilot of the Susquehanna.

Another time, while steering a pair of rafts for another pilot, the river being very high and wild and bearing us along with a tremendous velocity, after a long and hard day's run, we attempted to land for the night at Skinner's eddy. But that land-ing, which is usually good and safe, being pretty full of rafts already, we were kept out in the strong current, and under such headway that we did not make a success of it, but were hurried on our course in spite of all our efforts to land.

It was early in the month of March, and we had had alternate showers of rain, hail, and sleet, all day, which, together with a cold, raw wind from the north, made it very uncomfortable indeed. On trying to land, we had taken off our coats and put them in the cabin to keep them as dry as possible, and as the next landing was six miles below, on the opposite side of the river, and having a hard pull across to reach it, we let them remain there. It soon became so dark that we could not see the shore on either side, and before we knew that we were near shore, crash went the forward end of our right-hand raft, upon a sloping, rocky point which projects into the river a short distance above the landing. The shock was so heavy as to break the two rafts apart, and cause the one that struck to swing around and change ends, which had the effect to crowd the other out into the river so far that it passed to the left of a small island that lies directly in front of the landing. The pilot remained on the cabin raft, which swung round near the shore, and easily succeeded in getting into the eddy and landing it safely. I had charge of the other with only one man to assist me, and he entirely without experience, this being his first trip down the river, and we had no shelter from the drizzling sleet, which still continued, and not even our coats to keep us warm; surrounded by Egpytian darkness, we could see nor hear nothing except the roaring of the mighty river, which was swiftly bearing us away upon its bosom, we scarcely knew whither. We might be running endwise, or lying across the current, and might keep the proper course through the main channel, or fetch up on some island upon the main shore. We had no means of knowing our true position, and any amount of work pulling to the right or left would not be likely to better our condition; but still we stood at our oars and waited for coming events.

All we knew was that we were going at a tremendous rate of speed, and that we would soon have to pass through a narrow and swift channel known as the Horse Race, between some islands and the main shore, and then around the horseshoe bend, and then, if we did not strike anything before, we had to run to Wilkesbarre Bridge, and at the speed we were going might reach Nonticoke dam before morning. This dam was a very high one, and the back water below it was so strong that it would roll up and completely destroy every raft that had the misfortune to run over it, and its shute was narrow and close to the left-hand shore. No one ever attempted to run it except in broad daylight. Our prospect just at that time was anything but pleasant.

We soon heard the dismal roar of the Horse Race, and my man had just come forward to inquire what it all meant, when I got a glimpse of the rocks on shore at our right and knew then that we were in the proper channel and running right end first. I sent the man back to his oar, telling him to keep her straight, but on reaching the hind end of the raft his oar was not there. The hind end of the raft had probably swung so near the rocks as to have caught the end of the oar stem, unshipped it, and carried it into the river. That was the only way that I could account for it at the time. (These oar stems are usually forty feet in length and one foot in diameter in the largest place, and the blade from twelve to sixteen feet in length, and two feet in width.)

The next dangerous place was the Horseshoe Bend, and we were soon there, yet had no means of knowing it. Here raftsmen always had to work hard to keep the raft from striking the shore in the sag, or outside of the circle. All this I knew very well; but not being able to see the shore, the first intimation that we had that we were in the bend, was the crash of the forward end of our raft upon the rocks on shore in the sag, which shivered the blade of our only remaining oar and brought us to a sudden halt; but before we could change the cable from the hind end to the front, and fasten to a small hemlock tree which grew near the water's edge, the raft, which had apparently been on the swing ever since it struck, suddenly slipped off the rocks and left us both on shore.

Upon examining our situation more at leisure, we found that we were upon a narrow strip of broken rocks, with a perpendicular wall of rocks which composed the base of a high mountain on one side, and the mad, roaring river on the other, close at our feet.

We tried to move up and down the river, but found it out of the question to do so in the darkness, as in places the river surged against the wall and barred our egress. Our only alternative was to find the best situation we could and wait for morning. So, perched upon the broken fragment of a rock, which had sometime fell into the edge of the water from the dark, frowning mountain above, with our backs leaning against the cold and dripping wall, completely exhausted and shivering with cold, and in imminent danger of falling into the river,

> "There we sat like those who wait
> Till Judgment seals the doom of fate."

It seemed almost an age, but daylight appeared at last, and as soon as we could move our stiffened limbs we began to cast about us for some means of escape. Below us was a deep cut in the mountain where a small creek came down to the river, and we thought if we could only reach that we could probably scale the mountain at that place. So, working our way as best we could, by sometimes hanging to the brush that grew out of the seams of the rocks above the water, and scaling huge bowlders that lay in our way, we succeeded at last in reaching the cut, and scaling the mountain to its top, where we found a clearing and dwelling house among the small pines, and were heartily welcomed by the inhabitants, and furnished with a good breakfast.

After relating our adventures and receiving the warm sympathy of our kind host and hostess, and their congratulations upon our escape, we were directed to a road which led down the mountain to a ferry, where we hired a boatman to take us aboard a fleet of rafts which were passing at the time, and diligently scoured the river on every side for our raft, which we finally discovered lying in front of the city of Wilkesbarre, safely tied to the shore.

A man who lived upon the bank of the river alone, had discovered it just at daylight that morning com-

ing down crosswise the river; had boarded it, and
with the help of others had succeeded in landing it,
for which service they charged us ten dollars. Our
pilot with the other raft soon came along-side us; we
joined him, and were soon under way.

MY LAST TRIP TO TIDE.

I had followed the river each spring during the
five years I attended school at the academy, and the
last three springs I had remained down the river and
steered through to tide, as long as the water remained
high enough, or while there was anything to run. I
had become accustomed to steer a raft safely through
among the rocky rapids and whirling eddies of the
lower Susquehanna, and never had met with an
accident or disaster of any kind, although we often
found the rocks on either side strewn with wrecks
made by those who were less skillful or less fortunate
than ourselves.

At the time of which I write, it was becoming
late in the season, the water low, and the lumber
nearly all through, when a noted steersman, who we
will call Jim Green, came to me and said he would
like to try his hand one trip as a pilot. He knew of
a raft he could get, and if I would agree to steer for
him, he would take the contract of running it
through. I readily consented on the conditions that
he would pay me the highest price for steering, and
take all the risk himself.

We started early the next morning, and got along
well enough until we came to a place known as Tur-
key Hill. Here my new pilot got headed altogether
too far to the right for the channel; and I told him
so; but he thought not, but finally came to the hind
end of the raft, and quickly discovered his mistake.
He returned to his post and tried hard to pull into
the channel, and I gave him all the headway I could;
but it was too late. We struck a huge rock at the
right-hand side at the entrance of the channel with

such force as to snap the couplings on one side of the raft, causing the raft to double up like a jackknife, and in that condition we struck another rock directly below, which entirely separated the two parts of the raft. The forward part, with the pilot and one man, swung round entirely out of the channel, went crashing among the rocks below, and finally drifted onto a ledge and remained fast. But my end of the raft, with four men besides myself, kept the channel until we reached Fry's Falls, when, not being able to get the proper headway, we drifted away to the right of Fry's Rocks, a long ledge lying nearly crosswise of the river. But getting into the eddy of this ledge, and using planks for additional oars, we worked our raft back into the channel and finally succeeded in landing at the mouth of Wilson Creek, just above Conestoga dam, where I ordered dinner for all hands, to which we did ample justice, and then hurried away up the river in search of our pilot.

We succeeded in finding his part of the raft, but not the pilot. He was not there, he had gone; a canoe had taken him ashore, and I never saw him more.

ON THE HOME STRETCH.

Raftmen usually returned home on foot, traveling up the main river and the West Branch, through the great State of Pennsylvania to Williamsport, thence across the Alleghany Mountains to Blossburgh, and thence down to the Shemung River, and up its various branches to the starting-point. Besides our regular wages down the river, we were allowed six days to return, and two dollars per day for wages and expenses. We usually made the distance (about two hundred miles) in five days hard travel, stopping at the hotels along the route for meals and lodging, where we were always well treated.

But sometimes when we thought we could afford it, we came around on rail and steamboat, *via* Philadelphia, New York, and Albany, where we could see the elephant and have a good time generally. And in this way I managed, at little cost, to see much of the world, both in city and country, and enjoyed a great variety of life and scenery.

IN THE HARVEST FIELD.

It was harvest time, and I had as usual laid aside my student's garb, consisting of a silk hat, fine clothes, and polished boots, and put on my farmer's rig, and had been in the harvest field long enough to wear the blisters off my hands, and harden my muscles for the work before me, when Colonel Post, upon whose farm I was engaged cutting wheat, with half a dozen other cradlers, came into the field near the close of the day, and observing that I handled a cradle very easily, offered to bet twenty-five dollars that that "Yankee boy," as he called me, could cut seventy dozen sheaves of wheat in a day. He said that he had seen an account in the papers of some one doing it in an adjoining county, and thought by the light and easy way I had of handling my cradle that I could do as much as any other man. At all events, he was willing to risk money on it. No one present seemed anxious to take the bet, but he told me that if I would undertake to win it for him, he thought he could get his bet taken up town.

The next morning the boss told me that the money was up, and that he would set apart a portion of the field where we were then working, and that I might have two binders, instead of one as usual, and that I might undertake it the next day. So, putting my cradle in first-rate order, I commenced soon after sunrise the next morning, and took an easy gait until I got warmed up to the work, and then went into the grain faster and faster; and before noon I was under good headway, and my two binders had all they could do to keep up with me. After dinner I commenced again at a pretty lively rate of speed, and

made it still livelier from that time till night, being
sometimes three or four times around the piece ahead
of my two binders, and would then go back and help
them bind till they caught up with me. I also helped
them set up the sheaves in bunches, and just as the
sun was going down we counted them and found that
we had one hundred and eleven dozen.

Just as I was leaving the field, with my binders
some distance behind, I met the Colonel, who eagerly
inquired if I had made the seventy dozen. I told
him we had and something over, I believed; but that
he had better ask the boys who had just finished
counting them. And when they told him that I had
cut one hundred and eleven dozen, he threw up his
hat and yelled like an Indian.

Here was glory enough for one day. Colonel Post
had my performance published in the county paper,
and the article went the rounds of the press in most
of the agricultural districts of the State. But my
hard-earned laurels could not be worn without envy.

There lived in the town of Lodi, Seneca County,
near the scene of my exploits, a man by the name of
Joe Brokaw, who was a stout, well-built man, and
claimed to be the bully cradler of the county. This
man was not only a great bully, but a great braggart,
and delighted in showing his great strength and
powers of endurance on every suitable occasion; and
being of a very mean and tyrannical disposition, very
few men cared to work with him in the harvest field,
for fear of being run down and "bushed," as it was
generally termed where a man had to give up and
quit the field before night, on account of weakness or
fatigue. He and his immediate followers declared
that no man could cut the amount of wheat that was
claimed for me in one day; and said that there was
either a mistake in the count or else the sheaves
were purposely made small, and would not yield a
bushel of wheat to the dozen, as was usually the case.
Forty dozen, they said, was a good day's work for

any man, and they did not believe the man lived who could cut the amount credited to me in one day in good, honest sheaves. They finally offered to put up a purse of one hundred dollars against an equal amount, that neither myself or any other man could cut one hundred dozen sheaves of wheat in one day that would yield a bushel to the dozen.

Colonel Post, after advising with me, and procuring my consent, finally agreed to take the bet. But as the wheat harvest was nearly over for that year, the time was deferred to the next harvest.

The next year I was on hand as usual, and was shown a field of five acres of wheat not yet ripe. which Colonel Post told me he had put in with extra care, and was quite sure that it would yield over one hundred bushels, and asked me if I could cut it in a day. I told him I thought it would be an easy task, and that he could put up his money on it with perfect safety.

I went to work in fields where the grain was already fit to cut, with other men; and by the time the small field was ready, I was in excellent trim for cutting it. So one fine morning, having all things ready, and two good binders as before, I set about my task, and before noon was well satisfied that I had the field under easy control, and the sun was still an hour high when I had my task completed. and the sheaves all set up in dozens and counted, there being one hundred and fifteen dozen and a few sheaves over.

I offered to finish the day in another field, but the Colonel would not consent to it, as he said he was quite sure he had won the bet, and that we had done quite enough for one day. When the wheat was threshed, it turned out one hundred and seventeen and a half bushels. This defeat and the loss of their money made Brokaw & Co. madder than ever, and they swore that they would have revenge at any cost.

At that time many of the farmers in central New

York were in the habit of occasionally sowing large
fields to flax to be cut for seed. This was done par-
tially to relieve the ground from constant crops of
wheat, and then as flaxseed could always be readily
sold for cash, it generally proved a profitable crop
to raise. There was quite a nack in cutting it; but
when once perfectly understood, a man could cut
more acres of it in a day than any other crop raised.

Joe Brokaw and one of his associates by the name
of Bill House had contracted to cut a large field of
flax by the acre, for Colonel Smith, and sent me a
sort of challenge to come and work with them if I
dare, and at the same time offered to pay me two
dollars and a half per day. This was more than
twice the usual wages, and although I knew their
object was to use me up if they could, I at once determined to accept the proposition, and take the
chances. When my old friend, Colonel Post, heard of
it, he tried to dissuade me from going, telling me that
it was a trap set between the two to use me up, and
that they would have every advantage of me, as they
were old, experienced hands in cutting flax. while I
had never had much experience. But I told the
Colonel that I had had some experience, having
helped cut one small piece, and that I thought I could
hold my own with them at least, and as for their
tangling me up between the two, by not keeping
stroke, I knew a trick worth two of that. And besides every other consideration, it was now too late
to decline their challenge, as I had already accepted
it.

This affair caused considerable excitement in the
village of Lodi and the surrounding country, and
when the day arrived for the work to begin, quite a
large crowd visited the farm of Colonel Smith, to
witness the contest, among whom I noticed many
prominent citizens, and some ladies. I went down
to the farm early in the morning, and found Brokaw
and House already there, and breakfast not being

ready, and the field close by, we concluded to cut around a portion of the field before breakfast. So we took our cradles, which were all ready for service, and moved to the starting-point, near the barn. Brokaw offered me the lead at the first start, but I respectfully declined, and told him that as he was the best cradler we would confer that honor upon him, and I would take the rear. Without any more words he started ahead, and Bill House next down the side of the field next the road, until they thought they had got far enough for a day's work, when they came to a halt; and after sharpening our scythes, we started down across the field with Bill in the lead, myself next, and Joe took his place in the rear. Joe at once commenced to crowd upon me, and push me down upon Bill House, so that we worked all the way down across the field side and side. This gave me a good opportunity to measure strokes with them, and I found that I could make from one to two inches clean cut each stroke further than either of them, and that I had it in my power to cut Bill out of his swath at any time I chose.

On the lower side of the field, it was my turn to take the lead along the fence toward the house. Just as we were about starting, the horn blew for breakfast, but as we were then cutting towards the house, I suggested that we had better cut on through, as we would then have less distance to walk going and coming. To this they assented, and we started in, and as there was now no one before me, I took a steady stroke and gave my cradle all it could do, until I reached the corner of the field next the house, when I found that Joe and Bill had been left several rods behind, and, without waiting for them to come up, I got over the fence and went to the house, where I was received with every manifestation of delight. The gentleman who had charge of the farm told me that Brokaw had remarked that morning before I arrived, that "they intended to bush me that day or get a d—n big day's work out of me;" but it was the general impression that he was making rather a bad beginning.

I accepted that remark as a declaration of war, but knew that I had command of the situation, and at once determined to make the most of it.

On returning to the field after breakfast, I made it a point to press the man before me as close as the rules of the harvest field would permit, when in the middle or behind, and give my cradle every quarter of an inch it would cut, when in the lead. "*My motto was fair play, and let the best man win.*" But Joe Brokaw made several frantic efforts during the forenoon to crowd me upon Bill House, and then by breaking stroke tangle me up between their two cradles; but this plan did not work to their satisfaction, as I had a way of swinging my cradle back and forth in such a manner as to avoid a conflict with either of them.

At noon Joe complained bitterly that his cradle did not work well, and said that his scythe was dull, and requested Bill House and I to grind it for him after dinner, while he stretched himself out on the floor for a rest. By the time we got to work after dinner, people from the town and surrounding country commenced gathering at the house and along the roadside to see the sport, and by the middle of the afternoon there was quite a crowd assembled, in buggies, on horseback, and on foot.

I pursued the same course in the afternoon that I had so successfully pursued in the forenoon, and was soon satisfied that House was a better cradler than Brokaw, as by pressing him hard I could drive him away from Brokaw at any time, which would make him rave and curse like a pirate.

Matters went on in this way until about two hours before sundown, when, the piece that we went around in the morning being finished, Joe proposed to quit work, remarking that we had done enough work f one day, and that he was willing to pay me for a day's work; but I told him that I was not in the habit of quitting till sundown, and proposed to take a turn around another piece. To this proposition he very reluctantly assented, and we went down to the lower corner to cut up through towards the road, and now was my opportunity to make a display of skill and endurance.

It was Bill's turn to take the lead, and I came next, with Joe in the rear. And all the way up the side of the piece to the road I drove Bill before me, keeping about even with him, and whenever I was gaining too much, so as to bother him, I would quietly take my cradle on my arm and let him gain a stroke or two, and then at it again, while Joe was being left a long distance behind. This kind of tactics amused the crowd (many of whom had climbed upon the fence the better to see the performance) wonderfully, and long before we reached the road, we were greeted with mingled shouts of applause and derision. As soon as we had reached the fence, I went back to help Joe out; but, irritated beyond endurance by the jeers and taunts of the crowd of spectators, he smashed his cradle upon the ground, and quit the field, swearing that he would never cut another stroke while he lived. In about an hour Dr. Post was called upon to see Joe, and found him in a dangerous fit of cholic with spasms (caused, the doctor said, by over-exertion), and stayed with him during the night. He finally recovered, but was never known to use a cradle afterwards.

After this I was the *lion* of the whole county. Go where I would, I would hear it whispered among both men and women, *"That's the man that bushed Joe Brakaw."*

On hearing that there was a fifty-acre field of flax about five miles south of Lodi, I visited the place and took the contract to cut it at fifty cents per acre. When the time came to commence cutting it, I went up alone, and the owner told me that he thought I was going to have help or he would not have let me the contract. I asked him if his flax was suffering to be cut, and he answered that only a small part of it was fit to cut at present, but that much of it would be spoiled before I could cut it alone by myself.

I proposed to him that I would start in the next morning, and any time he thought any of his flax was likely to suffer for want of being cut, to let me know, and I would get help. To this he agreed, and in the afternoon of the next day he came into the field where I was working and seemed greatly surprised at the amount I had already done, and after taking a good look over the whole field, he walked up to me and asked, *"Ain't you the man that bushed Joe Brokaw, down at Lodi?"* I replied that such was the case. "I thought so," said he, "as soon as I saw your work; I have no fear now that you won't get it cut soon enough."

After finishing that job, I took a contract of another man to cut a field containing seven and a half acres, and finished it in one day, though I was expected to be two or three days at it.

MY LAST TERM AT SCHOOL.

IT is now nearly forty years since I was a student at the old Homer Academy, Cortland County, New York. The number of students at this school usually ranged from two hundred to three hundred, composed to a great extent of the sons and daughters of the inhabitants of the surrounding country; but as the school, under the able management of Professor Woolworth, was deservedly popular, many students came from a longer distance, and some even from the adjoining States.

At the time of which I write, besides Professor Woolworth, who heard recitations in some of the higher branches, there were three male and two female teachers employed; and there being no regular boarding-house belonging to the school, the students usually procured board and lodgings about the town, where accommodations could be had. Some only hired rooms, furnished with beds, stoves, and cooking utensils, sufficient for the accommodation of from two to four students, who desired to club together and do their own cooking, etc., as a matter of economy. The writer, being one of the latter class, usually had from one to three "chums" associated with him in the culinary department.

All lessons were studied at these rooms, and we only went to the academy building to attend lectures and prayers in the morning, and at set hours during the day to recite to the teachers at the several rooms which they occupied for the purpose of hearing the recitations of each class in its turn.

There were also three literary societies, or debating clubs, belonging to the institution, which were known respectively as the "Elihu Burritt Society," "Franklin Club," and "Council Fire." At the time of which I write, these three literary associations each elected three delegates for the purpose of forming a Board of Publishers, whose business it was to establish and print a small monthly paper, to be made up from original contributions by the students, and to be known as the *Students' Casket.*

Being one of the prime movers in this enterprise, I was elected one of the delegates, and finally president of the Board of Publishers. At the first session of the Board a rule was adopted, that each contribution for the columns of the paper should be read before the Board by its secretary, and submitted to a vote whether it should be received or rejected. The mechanical part of the work was to be done at the office of the old *Cortland County Whig*, then published in the village of Homer. The new paper altogether made a very creditable appearance, and very readily sold in town and among the students, for three cents per copy, which more than paid the cost of publishing. And as the students sent copies to their friends all over the county, by the time the second number was ready to issue, we had quite a long list of regular subscribers, and the little paper had every appearance of being a splendid success, and an honor to its founders, managers, and contributors.

Had the managers confined themselves to their legitimate business of publishing the paper as originally intended, everything would no doubt have gone on smoothly enough; but such was not the case. They had no sooner become popular with the school than they began to interfere with its rules and discipline.

In the first place the principal of the school, who was familiarly known among the students as "Old Pray" (or, in plain English, the old man that prays), had given orders that every student should be out at prayers, at the ringing of the bell at nine o'clock each morning. Many of the students took exceptions to this rule on the ground that it interfered with their studies, and then they could not see the necessity of leaving their warm rooms each cold winter morning, and going to the large, cold lecture room to hear "Old Pray" go through the same dry, monotonous jargon of words each successive morning.

Some had been severely reprimanded for not making their appearance as ordered, and the matter began to be very warmly discussed at the weekly meetings of the several literary societies, and finally reached the Board of Publishers, and cropped out in some of the contributions which were accepted for publication. And so matters went on, until one very cold morning it was generally observed that the bell did not ring as usual for prayers. The bell-ringer pulled on the rope and the bell went round as usual, but gave no sound. It was soon whispered around that some adventurous students carried two or three buckets of water up into the belfry the evening before and turned it into the bell. It had frozen solid during the night, and held the tongue of the bell to its place. The rule was somewhat relaxed after that affair, and quiet would soon have reigned once more, but suddenly an order came for the Elihu Burritt Society (which was the oldest and ablest literary club of the school) to vacate the room on the first floor, which it had occupied for years, and occupy one not nearly so large or convenient, on the second floor. This they absolutely refused to do, and, upon finding the door of their old room locked against them, hastily adjourned to meet in a hall which they had procured at one of the principal hotels. Here they made speeches, and passed resolutions which were anything but complimentary to the management of the school. The other societies made common cause with them, and the Board of Publishers being composed of delegates from each society, and its president a member of two of them, followed suit, as a matter of course, and carried a very large majority of the school with them. Indeed, it would not be exaggeration to say that these nine young men who composed the Board of Publishers, had at that time more power over the minds of the two hundred and fifty students who then composed the school than all the teachers, principal included—and I don't know but we might throw in the president and Board of Trustees, with perfect safety. We may have been wrong, but we believed we were right, and acted accordingly, which I hold is the only true and safe course to pursue in all cases of that kind.

We went regularly to our recitations as usual, and were perfectly orderly and respectful towards our teachers, as far as our various studies were concerned, but in other matters were at variance; and thus matters continued to the close of the term.

As the term drew near its close, arrangements were being made as usual for a grand public examination and exhibition. Each of the three literary societies promptly passed resolutions respectfully declining to have anything to do with the matter, and forwarded copies of the same to the principal teachers.

The faculty, however, after holding a consultation over the matter, concluded to go on in the regular routine, with such material as they could control, and do the best that lay in their power. There were some students of two or three years' standing who had never belonged to any of the clubs, and there were also many dissenters from the recent rulings of the clubs who, from prudential motives, decided to obey the wishes of their teachers, and were willing to do what they could to make the exhibition creditable; and so the preparations for the affair went on as usual.

Seeing that we were likely to be beat at last, we determined to have our share of the fun out of it at all events, and the evening before the close of the term, half a dozen of the leading spirits met at my room in complete disguise; and, after partaking of an oyster supper which my chum and I had prepared for them, and charging my chum to keep the hall door unbolted, so that I could get in at any time during the night, we left for the suburbs of the town in search of an adventure.

Coming to a small field where there were three or four old Merino rams with big, winding horns, securely fettered for safe keeping, we seized upon the largest and most formidable looking one of the flock, and, releasing him from his fetters, led him captive into the heart of the town and public square, where the academy buildings and principal churches were situated. As it was the rule for all doors to be closed and securely bolted at precisely ten o'clock at night, and it now being as late as eleven or twelve o'clock, there was no one stirring.

As all the outside doors of the school buildings were found to be securely locked or bolted, some of us firmly held the prisoner, while others went for a long ladder not far away, where a house was in process of rebuilding, and with this one of us succeeded in entering the building through one of the second story windows, and soon had the front door open to admit the captive, whom we led in through the hall and up the stairs to the lecture room, where the exhibition was to take place. Here we turned him loose, and after bolting all the doors as we found them, and fastening down the windows except the one we went out at, "we left him alone in his glory," and, after taking the ladder back where it belonged, returned to our several lodgings.

But what was my surprise and chagrin when I found the doors of my own apartments securely barred against my admittance. I scarcely knew how to account for my chum's neglect; could it be possible that he had thrown off on me and thus betrayed me into the hands of my enemies? I could not believe it for a moment, but nevertheless it was a stern fact that if I did not succeed in getting into the house, I would surely be reported the next morning as absent during the night, and all the mischief done would be laid directly to my charge. The prospect was anything but pleasant, but what could I do? I dare not make a noise and arouse the house; for that would expose my guilt, and lead to my disgrace and that of my comrades at once.

I sat down upon the door-step and surrendered my mind to the deepest and most intense train of thought, but could see no way of getting out of the difficulty except by getting into the house. Is it possible, I thought, that every door and window is securely fastened? There was a small window under the eaves at the head of the stairs which opened horizontally, that might not be fastened—all the others I knew fastened with springs whenever they were closed. I must try that window, I thought; but how can I reach it? I thought of the ladder we had used at the academy.

Taking off my hat, coat, and boots, I laid them carefully upon the door-step, and, with as little noise as possible, went for the ladder, which, with some difficulty on account of its great length, I brought and reared against the eaves of the roof, and was soon up at the window, the sill of which I could just manage to reach by poising myself between the rounds of the ladder, when to my great joy I found that the sash moved at my touch, and I was soon inside the house. I then went carefully down-stairs to the hall door, which I unbolted and opened with the least noise possible, and, after carrying back the ladder to the place where it belonged, I took my coat, hat, and boots, bolted the door as I had found it, and went quietly up-stairs to my room.

I was so elated with my escape and the adventures of the night generally that I could not sleep a wink that night. It was yet quite early in the morning when our landlady made her appearance at the head of the stairs, and called to my chum, who was still in bed, remarking that *she guessed she had Schofield this time.* But before he had time to answer, I growled from my room, "*I guess you hain't,*" at which she slumped down the stairs without another word.

My chum then told me that the old lady had sat up most of the night watching that door, and that he had slipped down three times during the night and unbolted it; but each time she had been on the watch and bolted it after him, and, while waiting for her to go to bed, he had himself fallen asleep, and thus it was that I found the door bolted.

Professor G., who had the immediate supervision of the preparations for the exhibition, was a vain, dressy little man, with any amount of self-conceit and aristocratic notions about him, and as the last private rehearsal before him was to take place at half past eight o'clock, I got my breakfast and repaired to the academy to watch developments. Professor G. was already there with about a dozen students, trying to get into the hall; and, on finding the doors securely bolted and the windows fastened down, he sent for a stick of wood, with which he hammered away at one of the doors till the bolts gave way and the door flew open. In the meantime the old ram had watched the progress of events, and was ready for a charge for liberty, as soon as he should see an opening. The professor saw the old patriarch, with head erect and eyes of fire, dropped his club, and commenced a precipitate retreat, but was too late. He had no sooner turned to run than the enemy made a terrific charge on his flank and rear, and hurled him prostrate to the floor, and at the same time catching the end of one of his horns in one of the pockets of his swallow-tailed coat, he ripped it from the tail to the collar. Then leaving him more scared than hurt, he rushed through the hall to the head of the stairs (the students clearing the way for him by rushing into the recitation rooms on each side of the hall), then down the stairs he rushed with the velocity of a cyclone into the lower hall and then out the front door into the public square. Old Pray was just coming up the front steps as the ram dashed down, but he stepped aside just in time to avoid a collision, but was badly scared, and whooped like a wild Comanche. As most of the school was present by this time and the bell was ringing for prayers, we all went in to see what the old man had to say. He gave us a pretty severe lecture, expressing his sincere regrets at what had taken place, and closed by dismissing the exhibition and the school for the term.

I afterwards learned that a reward of twenty-five dollars was offered by the trustees, to be paid to any one who would make known any of the perpetrators of the deed; but every one was true "to his trust."

NARRATIVE OF A CALIFORNIA PIONEER.

INTRODUCTION.

THE author left his father's home
  With half a dozen more,
    And with the pioneers did come
To the Pacific shore.

They left the country of the lakes
  In the Great Empire State;
Their friends had furnished them the stakes
  With which to try their fate.

In eighteen hundred forty-nine
  They came across the plains,
O'er mountains, hills, and valleys fine,
  Through sunshine, snow, and rain.

NARRATIVE.

To Pittsburg first we took our way,
  Then through the mighty West;
At St. Louis awhile did stay
  Our money to invest.

We here procured a good supply
  Of things for camping out.
At Boonville we our teams did buy,
  Then started on our route.

We met the Sioux upon the Platte,
  Five hundred lodges strong;
They did not try to drive us back,
  But kindly cheered us on.

The chief with warriors at command,
  And women not a few,
With all the emigrants shook hands
  And shouted, "How-de-do?"

The war-chief sitting on his steed,
  A charger strong and true,
Did not to us a sermon read,
  But spoke as Statesmen do:

"Quite welcome are our pale-faced friends
  From the bright rising sun;
Quite welcome to our hunting grounds
  Are each and every one.

"When the great bison we pursue,
  We have enough to eat,
And now are glad to share with you
  Their most delicious meat.

"Turn out your teams, we will them feed,
  And guard your wagons, too;
We are prepared for every need,
  In friendship we are true.

"We sometimes fight Pawnees and Crows,
  For they our lands invade
And drive away the buffaloes,
  Which for the Sioux were made,

"But never shed a drop of blood
  Of our great friends, the whites,
For they to us are always good
  And give us all our rights.

"Go now, your happiness pursue.
  Our daughters, they are fair,
And to our lodges welcome you.
  They have not much to wear,

"But they are kind, and you are brave.
  Our sons are brave and true,
They will share anything they have.
  Good-night, my friends.   Adieu."

I watched some lovely girls at play
  Close by upon the green;
The war chief came along that way
  And marked the lovely scene.

"Bathilda," the great chieftain cried,
  "Come here, my child divine."
He led his daughter to my side
  And placed her hand in mine.

He bade me welcome to his home,
 He would his daughter give,
And I should a great chief become
 And always with them live.

The girl was tall and full of grace,
 Her dark eyes pierced me through,
And for awhile I must confess
 I knew not what to do.

Her dress, close-fitting, clean, and neat,
 Her skirts with beads were hemmed;
The small white slippers on her feet
 With beads were neatly trimmed.

   ———

Too soon I left my girl behind,
 Ahead were fields of gold;
Next morning at our starting time
 Our wagons westward rolled.

We crossed the branches of the Platte,
 The Rocky Mountain range,
And traveled down the western slope,
 A country wild and strange.

At length we reached the great Salt Lake
 'Mid mountains capped with snow,
And as I had some time been sick
 I could no further go.

The Mormons, led by Brigham Young,
 Had come the year before,
And found at last a quiet home
 By the great Salt Lake shore.

A city they had founded, too,
 And temple large and strong,
Greater than that at old Nauvoo,
 By far more broad and long.

They could run water where they pleased,
 All through the new-made streets,
Where they had planted young shade trees.
 The town looked fresh and neat.

We camped upon the grassy plain
 A short half mile from town.
The Mormons, hoping they might glean
 News from the East, came down.

We answered all their questions true,
  And asked as many more;
Some from the gold fields had come through
  With samples of the ore,

Which Brigham Young had folded up
  In papers strong 'and neat,
On which his priestly seal he put.
  With coin they did compete.

But very little goods they said
  Were in the new city;
The men there no tobacco had;
  The women wanted tea.

That they had plenty beef and ham,
  Milk, butter, bread and cheese,
And if we would take tea with them
  They would be greatly pleased.

Now we had with us plenty tea,
  Which none of us did crave,
As we preferred to drink coffee,
  So tea we freely gave.

I sought the house of Elder Pratt,
  His seven wives were there;
All one man's wives, so they did state,
  All healthy, fat, and fair.

I asked them how it came about,
  And to explain the plan
By which so many women stout
  Could put up with one man,

And told them where I used to live,
  'Way back in the far East,
The man who more than one did have
  Was treated as a beast.

They said that many women East
  From virtues' ways did fall,
Better one-seventh part at least
  Than have no man at all.

And Elder Pratt was very fair,
  All did his praises speak,
For each wife had his special care
  One day in every week.

I on that point no more did say
  While I with them did sup,
They thought they had the better way,
  And so *I* gave it up.

————

My comrades soon were on their way
  And left me quite alone,
For I had fevers every day
  And could not well go on.

A doctor came down to my camp,
  He did no physic bring,
But told me I must take a tramp
  Up to their famous spring,

And if I there would take a bath,
  After the second day
I would no chills and fever have,
  And could go on my way.

He said he learned the healing art,
  And used to purge and bleed;
But now to heal the sick was part
  Of his religious creed.

I thanked him for his kind advice,
  And told him I would try
The magic waters once or twice,
  And on his skill rely.

I went next morning to the place
  And found the waters warm,
And though I own I had no faith,
  A bath could do no harm.

And just the time I felt the worst
  I plunged into the pool,
Which seemed to me quite hot at first
  But afterwards more cool.

My bones stopped aching, cold chills ceased,
  No fever came that day;
I spent two hours in perfect peace,
  Then dressed and walked away.

I no more chills and fever had,
  Though I was very weak,
And for some days I kept my bed,
  Yet I could sleep and eat.

A farmer came along one day
  Who lived twelve miles up north.
He said he was from Ithica,
  Close by *my* place of birth,

And said the feed out at his place
  Was better for my mules,
Besides I would not there transgress
  The stringent city rules.

He had a wife and daughter fair,
  And two fine strapping boys.
The women could my food prepare
  And much enhance my joys.

Besides, as he was going east
  As far as the Black Hills,
I could *their* happiness increase
  By guarding them from ills.

I found his house upon the plain,
  Not far from the lake shore,
And there I did my strength regain,
  And was myself once more.

I found the Mormons kind indeed,
  They gave me every aid,
And loaned me Mormon books to read
  Through all the time I stayed.

I read the "Book of Mormon" through,
  The "Acts of Brigham Young,"
How Joseph died at old Nauvoo,
  His people shot and hung.

But riding out with Mary Jane
  Was what amused me more;
We often skimmed along the plain
  Or galloped on the shore.

She said she rode a thousand miles
  In coming to Salt Lake,
And had no fear of horses wild.
  She did wild horses break.

She did not like the Mormon creed,
  But said if during life
A husband did *her* wishes heed
  He would have but one wife.

But when her father back had come,
　I went with him one day
To make a call on Brigham Young
　And hear what he might say.

For he and I had laid our plans;
　In fact we were about
To search the streams for golden sands
　Along the southern route.

But Brigham sternly did forbid
　The aid and comfort sought.
" If there is gold 'tis better hid
　Than to the surface brought.

"Go home and cultivate your farm,"
　The stern dictator said.
" Go shield your family from harm
　And furnish them with bread.

" For if these settlements we leave
　And go in search of gold,
Our wives will soon with hunger grieve,
　Our children suffer cold."

So we could not our plans arrange,
　And I resolved to go
And cross the great Nevada Range
　Before the winter's snow.

As it was getting rather late,
　Most emigrants had gone,
I packed my mule, made matters straight,
　And started off alone.

But as I mounted for a start
　And bade my friends farewell,
Some words were said that touched my heart.
　These words I must not tell.

And when I camped on Webber's bank
　That night, though quite alone,
I found some things among my pack
　That made me think of home.

I had eight hundred miles to go,
　The Indians were bad,
As many pioneers well know,
　Who lost near all they had.
4

The moon was very near its full;
  The weather being clear,
The nights were very bright and cool
  That season of the year.

I rode by night and camped by day.
  Beacon fires gleamed far back,
The cougar screamed along my way,
  The wolf howled on my track.

Once as I rode till near daylight
  And reached the Humboldt fair,
Ahead I saw a camp-fire bright,
  And found two wagons there.

Two women only did I see
  There, sitting on the ground
Looking about quite anxiously
  And catching every sound.

I turned down to their lonely camp
  To see what I might see;
They quickly heard my horse's tramp,
  And gladly welcoméd me.

They said, an hour before day
  With fiendish yell and hoot,
The Indians drove their mules away, .
  Their men pursued on foot.

Right glad they were that I had come,
  And hoped that I would stay
Until their absent men came home,
  For *all* had gone away.

The men returned at close of day,
  But they no mules had found,
Save two which, pierced with arrows, lay
  Quite dead upon the ground.

Night came, I bade them all adieu.
  To go seemed almost wrong,
Yet there was little I could do
  To aid or help them on.

I hastened on, 'twas getting late,
  I never saw them more,
Nor learned what might have been their fate.
  Their chances though were poor.

On Humboldt River, quite far down,
　　I found a small pack train.
They said they were from Portland town,
　　Up in the State of Maine.

I told these gentlemen my plan,
　　And if we could agree
That I would join their little clan
　　And keep them company.

We reached the Humboldt sink all right
　　And stopped awhile to feed,
Then crossed the desert in the night.
　　We hastened through with speed.

Before we reached the Carson's tide
　　We saw a mournful sight,
Dead teams lay strewn on every side,
　　And wagons left and right.

Provisions were abundant there,
　　As flour and bacon too
Were left with wagons everywhere.
　　Their owners had gone through.

The Carson River has its charms—
　　Its valley long and wide
Lies nestled in Nevada's arms,
　　As lovely as a bride.

Now we wind up the mountain's side,
　　Through cañons rough and steep,
Often so steep we cannot ride
　　Or even keep our feet.

At last we reach the summit wide
　　And find deep banks of snow,
Until we cross the great Divide, 　·
　　Where we can look below.

Like Moses on Mt. Pisgah's height,
　　I viewed the promised land,
And what a boundless, peerless sight
　　Was there at my command.

Way down almost beneath my feet
　　A crystal lake was seen,
And then, to make the scene complete,
　　A forest vast and green.

And farther down more gentle hills
  The western slope did bound,
Though deeply cut by mountain rills,
  Beyond was open ground.

A mighty river from the north
  Flowed through a valley wide,
Another met it from the south.
  Both met the ocean tide.

The Coast Range rising farther west,
  A hundred miles away,
Hid from my view the ocean's breast
  And San Francisco Bay.

While thus each lovely scene I traced,
  My comrades all had gone
Far down to find a camping place,
  And I must hasten on.

We soon were camped at Weaverville
  Among the Central mines,
And fondly hoped, though void of skill,
  Our fortunes we might find.

We took a day or two to look
  And learn what others did,
But found no knowledge, art, or book
  Could show where gold was hid.

One man would venture on a claim
  And might a fortune find;
Others would venture just the same
  And come out far behind.

Some worked at least a dozen claims,
  With energy and skill.
Their luck was every time the same,
  They could not pay their bills.

We started in to find a mine,
  And worked a month or more;
But at the end of that long time
  Had little gold in store.

The clear, cool days of autumn passed,
  The winter storms had come,
And I was taken sick at last
  With scarce a house or home.

But when I better had become,
  I had resolved to try
And find at least a better home,
  A shelter from the sky.

I started out to find my horse,
  Left on a ranch below,
And thought I could not do much worse
  Wherever I might go.

But I had failed to find my horse,
  My money was all gone;
I had, to make the matter worse,
  Nothing to live upon.

Bacon and flour all around,
  But quite out of my reach.
They were a dollar each per pound,
  And meals two dollars each.

I found a hotel underway,
  Where I had camped before,
And told the landlord I would stay
  With him a week or more.

Said he, "There near the fire-place
  You spread your blanket down.
The man that occupied that place
  Is on his way to town.

"And as for grub, kind sir," says he,
  "That for itself will speak,
And then our charges, sir, will be
  An ounce and half per week."

I did his kindly terms accept,
  For what else could I do?
And now the next thing was to get
  The cash to pay when due.

A stranger came in late that night
  And said he was that day
In a fine valley, feed was high,
  And stock was fat and gay.

He thought no person claimed the ground,
  Or scarcely there had been.
High hills inclosed it all around,
  A river flowed between.

I asked the distance and the route.
  He carefully replied,
And took a coal and marked it out
  Upon the chimney side.

My mind was made, I had resolved
  A rancher I would be.
The deep, dark puzzle I had solved
  And now my mind was free.

I asked for paper, pen, and ink,
  Which soon were brought about,
And, after taking time to think,
  I carefully wrote out:—

" Notice, to all who come this way
  With stock to ranch or sell,
I will receive them every day
  Right here at this hotel."

I carefully the notice scanned
  And read it o'er and o'er.
The landlord took it from my hand
  And nailed it on the door.

Some men who stopped at the hotel,
  And those who passed that way,
Each saw my notice, read it well,
  And all agreed that they

Would leave their cattle in my hands
  And home return that day.
But scarcely spoke about my lands,
  Or what they had to pay.

One man had lost three yoke of steers.
  All day he hunted round,
But yet no hides, or horns, or ears
  Of them he yet had found.

If I would find the cattle lost,
  And take them home with me,
He said that he would pay the cost,
  And fifty dollars free.

A man from Placerville came there
  With cattle not a few,
Who thought my prospects would compare
  With any man he knew.

Thus cattle rapidly did come,
  And mules and horses, too.
I had a prospect of a home
  And plenty work to do.

I started with them that same day
  But did not get clear through,
For when I got about half way
  Those lost steers came in view.

The feed was good. I turned around
  And went back for the night,
And told my friend what I had found.
  He paid the cash on sight.

Next day I started out again,
  Prepared to stay all night;
I did that day the valley gain,
  And found my ranch all right.

That night I slept beside a trail.
  A grizzly bear came by,
And made a most terrific wail;
  I wished that I could fly.

It was too late to climb a tree,
  I covered up my head.
He snuffed and growled awhile at me,
  And gave me up for dead.

He was as large as any ox,
  Would weigh twelve hundred pounds,
And just as cunning as a fox.
  He nightly went his rounds.

———

A chieftain came to me next day,
  He was the capitan.
In broken Spanish he did say:
  Of a once mighty clan,

His mighty hunters all were dead,
  His people very poor.
His women though could work, he said,
  And wash the shining ore.

If I would bring them flour and meat,
  They all would come and buy;
Then they would have enough to eat;
  If not, they all must die.

Your cattle we will guard with care,
  And you shall be our friend,
And live in safety with us here.
  On this you may depend.

We cannot go away to trade,
  We dare not venture out;
Of white men we are much afraid,
  For many have been shot.

I went to try what I could do
  Up at the little town;
I got some flour, and bacon too;
  Next day I packed it down.

My trade was lively, pay was good.
  That nothing should be lost,
I charged my customers for goods
  Just twice what they had cost. .

They brought the gold-dust they had found.
  I weighed it out with care,
And gave them just as many pounds
  As they had dollars there.

I paid a man, to build a house,
  One-half an ounce per day;
But timber being good and close,
  We met with no delay.

My herd was growing very large,
  And, to keep matters straight,
I six per month for cattle charged;
  For horses I charged eight.

There was stray stock upon the ground
  When I located there,
And hundreds more soon came around,
  Which much increased my care.

From men who found their stock with me,
  And came that stock to claim,
I always charged a month's ranch fee,
  No matter when they came.

As many came to hunt stray stock,
  And often found it there,
Some were inclined to make a talk,
  Though everything was fair.

For cattle which can go at will,
　From mountains clad with snow,
At first will seek the river hills,
　Then work their way below,

Until they find abundant feed
　In valleys warm and low;
When they are satisfied, indeed,
　They will no farther go.

————

Two hunters came to me one day,
　To hunt *my* grizzly bear.
Among the hills, not far away,
　I pointed out his lair.

They followed up a large ravine,
　And, nearly at its head,
They saw where the great bear had been,
　And tracked him to his bed.

The brush was very thick and tall,
　They could not stand erect;
So on their hands and knees they crawled,
　His lodgings to inspect.

They held their guns with steady care,
　And kept their eyes ahead;
At the first sight of the great bear,
　They meant to shoot him dead.

The bear, in going to his bed,
　Had doubled and turned back,
And lay there sleeping, with his head
　Close to his former track.

And they, unwittingly, had crawled
　Close to his bearship's nose.
He gave a most unearthly squall,
　And on his haunches rose.

The hunters said they saw the bear,
　And heard his fearful yell;
Quick from his presence they did tear,
　But how, they could not tell.

They lost their hats and tore their clothes;
　Their guns they left behind;
Their faces redder than a rose;
　Their eyes with sweat were blind.

A few days after that affair,
A dozen men came down.
They came to hunt that same old bear;
Each had a knife and gun.

One boasted of his gun, and said,
"Now just give me a sight,
And I will kill that bear so dead
That there will be no fight."

Their leader was a mountaineer
Of much experience,
And grimly smiled this boast to hear—
He was a man of sense.

They went up to the hunting-ground,
And found the bear at home;
The leader placed his men around
At points the bear might come,

But told the man with the fine gun,
"As we are brave and stout,
We two will in the thicket plunge,
And route the monster out."

They started on two sides at once,
And moved along with care,
And though they did not far advance,
They roused him from his lair.

The bear upon his hind feet rose,
To see which way to run,
And chanced to be alarming close
To him with the fine gun.

He raised his gun, it was not cocked,
He could not hold it still,
Besides, he had not set the lock,
It would not go at will.

He dropped his gun, and gave a yell,
A shriek of wild despair,
And leaped the brush; you could not tell
Scarce where his foot-prints were.

The bear had counted up his foes,
And planned a quick retreat;
So down the rugged hill he goes,
And swam the river deep.

Each hunter claimed he pierced his hide
　With many shots before
The bear had reached the other side.
　I never saw him more.

A hunter came to live with me.
　The deer were thick and tame;
Almost without an effort, he
　Kept me supplied with game.

I charged an ounce per week for board,
　And paid an ounce each deer.
To pay that price I could afford,
　As shortly will appear.

The Indians and miners round
　Bought venison and beef,
And paid me fifty cents a pound—
　This was a great relief.

Sometimes my hunter killed a bear,
　Which he would pack around
And sell to miners everywhere,
　One dollar for each pound.

Bear meat sold high, for it was rare.
　I did not like bear meat;
But nothing scarcely will compare
　With stew made of bears' feet.

Sometimes he killed a bear alone;
　Sometimes I went along.
Sometimes he wanted only one,
　Sometimes a dozen strong.

One day he saw a mother bear
　Upon a hill-side nigh,
And well he knew a nest was there;
　He heard a young one cry.

We all turned out to see the fun,
　And bring the young bear home.
At the first shots the old bear run;
　We must have hurt her some.

I took the young one up with care,
　And with him joined the chase,
Not fearing that the mother bear
　Would her footsteps retrace.

The young bear cried, but we rushed on
  Upon the old one's track.
The fear of certain death alone
  Kept her from coming back.

To raise our little pet we tried,
  But he was very young.
For want of better care he died.
  This hurt my conscience some.

We later found another nest
  Hid in a lime stone cave;
And this stronghold we did invest,
  And did two young bears save.

————

My family was growing large,
  Stockmen, and miners too;
And the whole native tribe in charge,
  Their daily rations drew.

The winter storms held up at last,
  And gentle spring came on,
And everywhere was plenty grass
  For stock to feed upon.

I moved my herd out on the plains,
  Where everything was fresh
From being washed by winter rains.
  My cattle gained in flesh.

I found a lovely valley there,
  The natives called Bautuck;
No place could be more rich and fair.
  I thought myself in luck.

Rich fields of clover there I found,
  And kept the stock away.
I had resolved to claim the ground,
  And cut the grass for hay.

I went to San Francisco Bay,
  And bought a house all framed,
Which had been shipped out all the way,
  Clear from the State of Maine.

And this, in a short time, I did
  Erect upon a mound,
From which a splendid view I had
  Of all the country round.

But now my troubles did increase;
  The Mormons claimed the spot,
And would not give me any peace,
  But thought to drive me out.

They said that they had claimed the ground,
  And herded horses there;
And though they had not since been round,
  It still was in their care.

I told them I had built a house,
  And held possession there;
And if they meant to drive me out,
  To sail in if they dare.

Who were these Mormons I defied?
  Their camps here then were strong,
And they were all well armed besides,
  And backed by Brigham Young.

Some had been soldiers in the war;
  The roughest of their clan,
Their leader, the great murderer,
  Chief of the tribe of Dan.

I rode with Rockwell all one day,
  But did not know him then,
Nor did the Danite chief know me
  Until we met again.

He told me what a fearful strife
  The Mormon people had,
And how they had to fight for life,
  Against all who were bad.

That he had seen a hundred fights,
  And nearly always won.
The Mormons had maintained their rights,
  Their enemies had none.

For God, through Smith, had shown his will,
  And to his saints had given
The earth, with power to take and kill,
  And make a Mormon heaven.

And all who wish to save their lives,
  And live in peace at home,
Must take their property and wives,
  And to the Mormons come.

He was a dark, stern-visaged man,
  Well armed, as I could see,
A holster pistol at each hand,
  A large knife at each knee.

He looked as one born to command;
  And when he thought it right,
He was prepared to take a stand
  And make a bloody fight.

———

To drive me out, they never tried;
  I had too firm a hold,
And quite too many friends, besides,
  True friends, as good as gold.

But I soon found out, at my cost,
  That there was something wrong,
That cattle were quite often lost,
  And horses good and strong.

While stopping at Salt Lake I learned
  That Mormons sometimes steal,
And though the charge they often spurned,
  Its truth they made me feel.

Cattle and horses disappeared.
  We sought without delay,
But very seldom of them heard;
  They did not go astray.

The Mormons sometimes would pretend
  To look for stock astray,
And if not ready to defend,
  They drove large herds away.

But I was not alone, it seems,
  And company is good;
They often proved stock from the teams
  That freighted on the road.

They went in squads of four and six,
  And, when they met a team,
Some one part of the stock would pick,
  The others prove the same.

For these the teamster had to pay,
  For, whether false or true,
If half his stock was proved away,
  He could no farther go.

Once, while on business far away,
  Up at a mining town,
My trusty herder came to me
  And said a band had gone.

Some men had taken them by day.
  He tried to drive them back;
They sternly ordered him away.
  At night he lost the r track.

Six days I rode and searched and talked—
  This was a costly band—
For I had to produce the stock,
  Or pay upon demand.

I cursed Port Rockwell and his crew,
  And hunted every day.
At last of them I got a clue,
  About ten miles away.

Their herder left when he saw me—
  I did not learn his name—
But quickly drove the stock away
  Back to the ranch again.

A friend next morning came to me,
  Who said, " You better go
Away a little while, and see
  If times will smoother grow,

" For Rockwell took an oath last night
  That he would shoot you dead
The first time that he got a sight.
  He will do as he said.

" He does not take an oath in vain.
  Without fear or remorse
A hundred men at least he's slain.
  Come, saddle up your horse."

I told my friend I did not feel
  Like fleeing far from strife;
I would not turn upon my heel
  To save my own dear life;

That I would saddle up my horse,
  And back with him would go.
To me it seemed the better course
  At once to meet the foe.

"My friend," said he, "do stop and think,
　And grant me this request.
Do go, if only for a week;
　You need some little rest."

I will not flee from any man,
　Not for one single hour.
Within his fortress I will stand,
　And challenge Rockwell's power.

A brave man cannot die but once;
　A coward dies each day.
Am I a coward and a dunce
　That I should run away?

I have only one life to live,
　Only one death to die;
That life for rights I freely give,
　And all my foes defy.

I'll beard the lion in his den,
　Port Rockwell in his hold,
And if I die, farewell, my friend,
　Remember days of old.

I took my navy pistol true,
　And my good bowie-knife,
The safest instruments I knew
　In a contest for life,

And, mounting my most trusty steed,
　Alone I rode away.
My friend, whose voice I would not heed,
　Declined to go with me.

Dismounting at the "Block House" door,
　I entered the bar-room,
And saw but one man, yet heard more
　Within the dining-room.

I asked if Rockwell was at home;
　He said that he would see,
And went into the dining-room.
　Now was the time for me.

Facing both doors I took my stand,
　The center of the room,
With my revolver in my hand,
　And watched for him to come.

The talk grew very warm indeed
   Within the other room.
I plainly heard the women plead
   With Rockwell not to come.

Full fifteen minutes by the clock
   I watched for him to come.
I plainly heard Port Rockwell talk, •
   And knew that he was home.

The conversation died away
   At last, I heard no more.
As for the man I sent away,
   I saw him out the door.

He said that Rockwell was not home,
   And would not be that day;
But it was only since I came
   That he had gone away.

But as I left, the thought occurred
   That he might watch for me,
And waylay me upon the road.
   I went another way.

Port Rockwell was by far too wise
   To be slain in a fight.
He took his victims by surprise,
   And shot them dead on sight.

This whole affair was quickly known;
   News went from door to door.
But Rockwell that same night had gone.
   I never saw him more.

He gathered all the stock he could,
   And quickly started out,
Not by the plain, well-traveled road,
   But a more private route.

At Carsons next we heard from him.
   He got into a fight
About some cattle, killed his man,
   And left *there* in the night.

He soon arrived at great Salt Lake,
   Where he was a great man,
And did his old position take
   As leader of his clan.

5

The Indians had taken arms
  Against the Mormon rule,
But Rockwell, used to war's alarms,
  Soon did their ardor cool,

And, when our Government had sent
  An army to Salt Lake,
Port Rockwell, on resistance bent,
  Did every effort make.

He fortified each canyon well,
  Which to the valley led,
And managed his small force with skill.
  He stern resistance made.

He harassed Johnson and his troops,
  And captured army trains,
Which caused the army to lay up
  At Bridger, on the plains,

Until great Brigham gave consent
  To let our soldiers come
Into the valley, pitch their tents,
  And make themselves at home.

Now for a time I lived in peace,
  And cut my clover hay.
My herd had constantly decreased,
  Till all had gone away.

I sold my hay upon the ground,
  Which was soon hauled away,
Supplying all the taverns round
  With splendid clover hay.

Some men who came from the Coast Range,
  The region of Clear Lake,
Said they had cattle on the plains
  They wished to have me take.

They wanted to secure good range,
  Close by the mining towns,
That they with butchers might arrange
  To furnish beef all round.

They had about a thousand head,
  And when they could dispose
Of these, a thousand more they said
  They could bring if they chose.

Their stock was wild and full of fright,
  The wildest I had seen.
They were a most romantic sight
  When herded on the green.

And as the buyers picked them out,
  Vaqueros closed them round,
While others, with reatas stout,
  Would drag them to the ground.

The first would catch them by the horn,
  The second by the heel,
The third would sock the iron on,
  Until the hide would peel.

This brand, exactly like the old,
  Was only meant to show
That the poor creature had been sold
  And must to slaughter go.

Sometimes vaqueros showed their skill
  By throwing bulls alone.
His horse would hold the monster still,
  Till he was firmly bound.

I learned to ride in Spanish style,
  And throw the lariat,
And mounted horses tame or wild,
  Such as I chanced to get.

I had good horses not a few,
  And some of choicest breed.
I was a daring rider, too,
  And rode with reckless speed.

The antelope upon the plains
  Were swifter than the wind,
But when I loosed my bridle reins
  The greyhounds lagged behind.

I oft the antelope pursued,
  And chased him long and well,
Until, his fiery speed subdued,
  Into my hands he fell.

I knew a girl about eighteen,
  Tall, yet of faultless form.
She was as graceful as a queen;
  Her heart was pure and warm.

Her features bore the bloom of health,
  Her cheeks twin roses red,
And gentle dimples came by stealth
  For each sweet word she said.

Her hair was wavy, long, and dark,
  And floated loose behind.
Her dark eyes gleamed a gentle spark,
  Which showed a gentle mind.

She had most dainty hands and feet,
  Her voice was soft and low.
I fondly loved with her to meet,
  And with her riding go.

She had a noble pinto steed,
  That no one else might ride.
With her own hands she gave him feed;
  He carried her with pride.

We sometimes chased the shy coyote
  O'er hills and through ravines,
To places which were quite remote,
  Amid the wildest scenes.

The fairest blossoms on the plains
  Were not more fair than she,
And, when she held her bridle reins,
  An angel seemed to be.

Thus she and I in company
  Spent many happy hours,
For she was all the world to me.
  We often gathered flowers.

I loved her truly, long, and well,
  And deemed that she loved me.
Far better than her tongue would tell
  She loved my company.

But when I took her by the hand,
  And told her of my woe,
Unless I could her love command,
  She softly answered, "No."

We must not marry now, she said,
  Our lives are sweet and gay,
And I much fear that if we wed
  Our loves will pass away.

I did her sweet remonstrance hear,
  And bowed to her sweet will,
Yet did not from her presence tear,
  But loved her better still

And now, when years have rolled away,
  And youth and pleasure o'er,
I think she chose the better way,
  And love her still the more.

Although she did another wed,
  Though much against her will,
And has these many years been dead,
  I am her lover still.

A NEW DEPARTURE ON TEM-
PERANCE.

NEARLY forty years ago, while a student at the old Homer Academy, in the State of New York, in common with many other students, and some of the teachers, I united with the "Sons of Temperance," which was at that time comparatively a new institution.

Feeling the importance of the movement, and being at that time young and hopeful, I confidently believed that it would carry everything before it, and eventually overthrow the powers of old king alcohol, and emancipate all his slaves.

But although the same organization has continued to exist and labor ever since that time, and many other associations, having the same object in view, have from time to time come to its support, and although many of the States of our Union have from time to time enacted stringent laws for the suppression of the traffic in intoxicating drinks, and to prevent and punish the crime of drunkenness, and although the general Government has levied an enormous tax on intoxicating liquors of all kinds, so that they now cost many times their former price, yet, notwithstanding all these great and long-continued efforts to prevent the manufacture, sale, and use of intoxicating liquors, there are more consumed at the present time, in proportion to the population of the country, than there were forty years ago.

It is fully and conclusively shown by the statistics of the courts, and generally admitted by all parties who have taken the trouble to investigate the sub-

ject, that at least seven-tenths of all the crime, des-
titution, and misery in the country, is caused, either
directly or indirectly, by the use of intoxicating
drinks. And yet it has hitherto defied all the social,
moral, and legal powers of the country, to suppress,
or even check it in the least degree.

If we were to search for the true cause of this
great and ever-increasing evil, we would find that
nine-tenths of all the liquor consumed were drank by
persons who care very little or nothing about it, but
merely drink in conformity to a social custom, which
has been firmly established in this country, which is
simply treating each other as a mark of friendship
and respect. Very few, indeed, ever buy liquor and
go away by themselves to drink it, and the great
majority of those who drink care very little about
the kind of liquor, but will drink almost anything
that is most convenient, their whole object being to
show their respect and good fellowship for friends,
by treating and drinking with them, and thus comply
with the social custom of the country.

So we are at once led to the conclusion that it is
not the love of liquor, but this custom of treating
and drinking with each other, which has been so difficult to overcome. And, although there is a very
great difference in the amount of harm produced by
the use of strong liquors, such as whisky, brandy,
rum, and gin, and the more mild and less intoxicating
kinds, such as wine, beer, and cider, yet every movement in the cause of temperance has been aimed
alike at the whole line, from fiery whisky down to
poor, harmless cider.

Now suppose that the advocates of temperance
were to concentrate their forces against some particular point of old king alcohol's line of battle, instead
of continuing the attack all along the line at once,
what would be the result? Is it not reasonable to
suppose that by this means his lines could be broken,

and his whole force routed in detail?   In other words, suppose we suspend the contest against pure wine, beer, and cider, and have stringent laws enacted and enforced against the importation, manufacture, and sale of whisky, brandy, rum, and gin.   Such a course would not be at war with our established social cus-toms, and would at once enlist the wine-growing and beer-manufacturing interests of the whole country, as powerful allies in the cause of temperance and re-form, and thus insure a certain victory, which would eventually revolutionize the world.

The wine-growing interests of California are too powerful to be overcome.   The vines have taken deep root in the soil, and cannot well be removed, and I, for one, do not wish to remove them.   I rather wish to see our pure native wines take the place of stronger and more hurtful liquors, and be found in every house and on every table.   Their wise and moderate use will prove a blessing rather than a curse; and their production and sale will materially aid in making California the richest and fairest of the great sisterhood of States.

A SERMON ON POLITICAL ECONOMY—
1883.

"For unto every one that hath shall be given, and he shall have abundance; but from him that hath not shall be taken away even that which he hath."

THESE words, according to St. Matthew, were spoken in a spirit of prophecy, by the Saviour of mankind, nearly two thousand years ago, and very strikingly portray the state of our financial affairs in this country at the present time, which we will now endeavor to show in as clear and brief a manner as possible.

According to the present banking laws of the United States, any five or more citizens who are so fortunate as to be the joint possessors of $100,000, or more, can invest the money in United States registered interest-bearing bonds and deposit the same with the United States treasurer, and thereby secure the right and privilege of entering into a banking association; and the United States treasurer is authorized by law to give the new-made corporation ninety per cent of the amount of the bonds so deposited in United States bank notes, to be used as a circulating medium of exchange, with which to commence and carry on the business of banking.

These banks are taxed only one per cent upon the average amount of these notes actually kept in circulation, and one-half of one per cent upon their bank deposits and surplus capital. The bonds which they have on deposit with the United States treasurer are not taxed. By these arrangements it may be clearly seen that the bankers are enabled to make nearly

or quite fourfold interest upon the original amount
of money actually belonging to them: 1. By their
exemption from taxes upon the bonds they have on
deposit. 2. By the interest they draw upon these
bonds. 3. By the interest they receive on United
States bank notes, and their own checks and drafts
loaned out. 4. By interest and discounts from bank
deposits, besides many other means of making money,
best known to themselves.

Under the operations of this very beneficent banking system, according to the report of the secretary
of the treasury, there were, on the thirtieth day of
June last, 2,369 of these so-called United States
banks already established in different parts of the
country, with a capital stock of over five hundred
millions of dollars in the aggregate, and holding very
nearly that amount in United States bonds, upon
which they draw from eighteen to twenty millions of
dollars per annum from the Government in interest.
They also have over three hundred and twenty-four
millions of dollars in United States bank notes in
actual circulation, besides a much larger amount in
their own bank checks and drafts (which also circulate to a very great extent as a medium of exchange),
the interest upon which brings them another vast
harvest of gold.

It is not so easy to calculate the amount made by
them upon bank deposits and discounts, but, judging
from the nature of the business, it must be enormous.
Is it any wonder that millionaires multiply all over
the country with most astonishing rapidity? Bankers have no hesitation in exacting from five to eight
per cent interest on money loaned to merchants and
others, on good security, but they complain bitterly
about having to pay a tax of one per cent on the
United States bank notes furnished them by the
Government, and their own bank checks and drafts
are used by them in their business to a great extent

instead of United States bank notes, so as to avoid paying this tax as much as possible.

While the total currency of the country is very little short of $2,000,000,000, the United States bank notes in circulation are less than one-sixth of that amount, and all that the Government receives from these banks, from taxes and all other sources, is the comparatively insignificant sum of about $8,000,000 per annum.

At the same time there were $346,000,000 in United States treasury notes in circulation, which are now, and always have been, at par with United States bank notes. These notes cost the Government very little except the paper upon which they are printed. The gold and silver coin in the vaults of the United States treasury has, during the last three years, generally ranged from two hundred to two hundred and fifty millions of dollars. This large sum can easily be increased to any desirable amount and pledged to the redemption of these notes. And let it once be generally known to the public that there is constantly on hand in the vaults of the United States treasury a large amount of gold and silver coin which may be drawn upon at pleasure, by simply presenting the treasury notes at any of the numerous places of Government deposit, and very few would want the coin. Nearly all would prefer the treasury notes for the sake of convenience, and very little gold and silver would be required for general circulation.

And now we ask, in all candor, why, in the name of common sense, any considerable class of intelligent people, except bankers and their dependents, should desire to perpetuate this huge, complicated, and most

---

NOTE.—Since the above was written Congress has, with its usual generosity to the rich and powerful, repealed all the taxes on United States bank notes, surplus capital, and bank deposits, thus giving bankers $8,000,000 more.

expensive banking system. It may have been well enough at the time it was first inaugurated, nearly twenty years ago. The nation was at that time in the throes of a great civil war, a desperate struggle for existence. The Government had been forced to suspend specie payment, and experienced great difficulty in disposing of its bonds, so as to raise the necessary means for carrying on the war, and was consequently forced to offer very liberal terms to bankers, and others who had money, in order to secure their aid and co-operation in overcoming the difficulties with which we were at that time surrounded.

But these ends have now all been happily accomplished. Our glorious Union has been preserved, the honor of our flag vindicated, and the whole country has settled down into a state of peace and general prosperity. The bankers and money lenders have been made immensely rich as a fitting reward for their venture, and the banking system then inaugurated has already outlived its usefulness. The country now wants a financial system at once safe, cheap, and simple,—a system which will not require any very great amount of special pleading on the part of officers of the general Government in order to be clearly understood and appreciated by the people.

When the present banking laws expired by limitation, in June, 1883, would it not have been a master stroke of financial policy and sound economy to have substituted treasury notes for United States bank notes, now in circulation and in the hands of bankers, and thus redeemed the bonds now in the United States treasury as security for the banks, and thus by one grand sweep have canceled that large amount of our national indebtedness, and at the same time put an end to the payment of eighteen or twenty millions of dollars of the people's money, each year into the capacious vaults of the banks.

But Congress has already checkmated this movement, by rechartering these United States banks,
and there was no Jackson at the head of the Government, to put his veto upon this huge, overgrown
Polypus, which again threatens to capsize the great
ship of State.

We need but one kind of paper money, and that
should issue directly from the United States Treasury,
under the direction and general supervision of Congress.　This money would be perfectly safe, and can,
and should, always be kept at par with gold and
silver coin and circulate freely, without discount or
hinderance of any kind, from one corner of the Union
to another.

We are not among those who believe that congressmen are, as a general rule, any wiser or more honest
than the general average of their more humble
constituents.　It is well-known that many candidates
for congressional honors often resort to very question-
able means to secure their elections, and it need not
surprise any one that they should continue in about
the same course of conduct while in office, in order
to get back the money which they have already
expended, and more with it, so as to be the better
prepared for the next campaign, or for elegant retire-
ment.　Nor do Congressmen, as a general rule, live
much in the fear of God.　But, thanks to our wise
and good elective franchise, they do live somewhat in
the fear of the people, and as the good old Romans
used to say, "*Vox populi, vox Dei.*"　But it has been
truly said that in the multitude of council there is
safety, and as Congressmen are selected from among
the people of every section of the country in fair
proportion, they have better opportunities of knowing their wants and necessities, and are, therefore,
less likely to so regulate the currency of the country
as to cause stringency or inflation than bankers,
who, as a general rule, care only for their own private

interests, and pay very little heed to the wants and necessities of the people at large.

It may not be entirely out of place here to ask what Congress proposes to do with these pet banks. when the public debt shall be so far paid that there are no longer bonds enough left to answer the purposes of security for the issue of United States bank notes. Or does that honorable body propose to follow the recommendation of President Arthur, in his last annual message, and not be in too great a hurry about paying the public debt, so as to perpetuate the lease of bankers on the United States Treasury for an indefinite period, until all the wealth of the country shall pass into the hands of the banks and other rich and powerful corporations, and the great mass of the people become tramps and beggars, to be employed in flush times, at such wages as their lordly masters see fit to give them, and at other times to be locked out to starve, or wander from place to place, begging for employment and subsistence.

When a little money was wanted to pension the few surviving veterans of the Mexican War, who, by unsurpassed courage and endurance, shed so much glory upon the arms of our common country, and added six great States and Territories to the strength of the Union, there was no money for them. But when bankers ask for eighteen or twenty millions of dollars per annum, or a similar amount is wanted, ostensibly for internal improvements, but which will mostly find its way into the pockets of Government pets, there is money in abundance.

Nor are there any public lands to be distributed among the veteran soldiers of the late war for the Union, as a partial reward for the patriotism and valor displayed by them, in restoring the stars and stripes over each recreant State of our glorious Union. Yet within the last twenty years more than one hundred millions of acres have been donated to railroad corporations, which, in many of the States, through this Government aid, are fast becoming more powerful than the State governments themselves, and, if not checked, they will soon be entirely beyond State control, and, by uniting their forces, they may yet be able to grapple successfully with the general Government itself.

Neither has Congress made an appropriation for equalizing soldiers' bounties, or refunding what they lost by receiving a depreciated currency instead of gold and silver coin in scanty pay for their valuable services. But Congressmen take good care to see that their own services are well paid; they fare sumptuously every day, and many are enabled to live far above their salaries and still return to their constituents much richer than when they left.

It has been very difficult indeed for any class or association of poor people, however meritorious, to get any aid from Congress. That honorable body seems disposed to literally follow the spirit of the text: "Unto every one that hath shall be given, and he shall have abundance," etc.

The honorable members of Congress forcibly remind us of the good old deacon, who, being in very easy circumstances himself, his sympathies were very naturally with those of his own class and condition, and his daily prayer was, "Lord, help the rich, the poor can beg."

The old and very consoling theory of the ancient monks and hermits, that "those who were denied the pleasures and comforts of this world, and daily suffered for the bare wants and necessities of life, would have all the greater share of happiness and glory in the next," will hardly do for the people of this age and country. Nearly all feel as if they were justly entitled to a reasonable share of the good things of this world as they pass through it, and all the happiness and glory to which they may justly be entitled in the next world besides, and very properly question the right of any man or association of men, to monopolize an unreasonable share of the comforts and blessings which a munificent and just Creator has so bountifully bestowed upon all mankind. I repeat the question. Shall the few, through the aid and co-operation of Congress and the President, continue to accumulate their millions, and secure possession of the greater portion of the wealth of the country, while a much larger and more deserving class of citizens be made to suffer daily for the want of their just and rightful share of this wealth, which is securely held by the laws of the country, entirely beyond their reach? This all-important question must be finally settled by the people themselves at the polls, not in a single battle, but in a succession of battles, through all the coming years.

"Eternal vigilance is the price of liberty," and her champions must be ever on the alert; they must be ever active, vigilant, and brave.

We are largely in the majority, and if we continue to elect men to fill the various offices of the Government who will not serve our interests, it will be entirely our own fault. The remedy is clearly within our reach. We must organize, and discipline ourselves to act and vote together as one man, and always select our truest and best men for leaders, "and swear with them to hold the fort," and victory will perch upon our banners in every well-contested field.

A few more words and we are done with this branch of our subject.

Two objections are constantly being urged against the standard silver dollar. One objection is that it is too heavy and cumbersome for general circulation, while others contend that it is too light and should be made heavier, or, in other words, that they should contain more silver.

These two objections so nearly balance each other

that we should feel disposed to let them go for what they are worth, and drop the subject, but the late honorable Secretary of the Treasury, Sherman (and others have since followed his lead), states in his last annual report that the silver dollar did not contain a dollar's worth of silver, and recommended that the seventy-five or eighty millions then in circulation and in the vaults of the treasury should be recoined and more silver put into them.

Neither does a dollar treasury note contain a dollar's worth of paper. Yet it circulates at par with gold, and nobody wants it made larger so as to contain more paper. It is not the amount of material in the dollar that the people care for; but they want a dollar that will go for just one hundred cents, no more nor less. If the honorable secretary thinks that the standard silver dollar would circulate any better for having ten or fifteen grains more silver in it, we think he is very much mistaken. And there are also causes now at work, which, in all human probabilities, will create a considerable raise in the price of silver bullion before many years have rolled around, and should the honorable ex-secretary's recommendation be at any time put into operation, the mints would probably not get half through the heavy task of recoining before there would be a general demand that the amount of silver in the dollar should again be reduced.

It is always best to let well enough alone. Let the dollar of our fathers be also the dollar of our children. If the people prefer treasury notes for general circulation, by all means they should have them. Let the silver dollars remain in the vaults of the treasury till they are wanted. There is no possibility of getting too many of them on hand; and if the present vaults are not large enough, build larger ones. These dollars cannot be so easily stolen as gold coin or treasury notes.

6

It is in financial affairs as in war. In either case a strong reserve should constantly be kept on hand. And there should always be so heavy a resource of gold and silver coin in the United States Treasury that no combination of bankers, or other adverse circumstances, will ever again be able to force the Government to suspend specie payment, or make a corner in gold, and thereby cause a depreciation of the currency of the country. The present silver law should constantly be kept in force, and the mints continue to coin the standard silver dollar until silver bullion rises to such a figure that it can no longer be purchased and coined without loss to the Government.

We have now come to the consideration of the second clause of our text:—

"But from him that hath not shall be taken away even that which he hath" not.

Our revenue and banking systems are twin brothers in iniquity. The one takes from the poor, and the other, as we have already shown, gives to the rich. It is a simple truth that an Astor, or a Vanderbilt, or the wealthiest merchant in New York, pays very little more money into the national treasury (except as duties on goods, licenses, etc., which in the end is all paid back, and more with it) than any ordinary poor person.

And here comes the great puzzle, how to get money from a man that has none. It has been said that we cannot get blood from a turnip. The English Parliament solved this puzzle many centuries ago, and our Congress early got hold of the secret. These wise and cunning legislators do not wait for the money to get into the poor man's pocket; they would not trust him with it one minute. They cunningly contrive to get it before he gets his fingers upon it, or even sees it.

This is done by putting a tax upon nearly all of

the necessaries and comforts of life. This tax the
merchant pays, and adds to the original price of each
article of merchandise, with a good round sum besides, as profits and insurance against loss. The
merchant knows that the poor consumer must have
the goods at any cost, and he is right. The consumer buys the goods from the merchant, and foots
the whole bill. The money originally paid into the
United States Treasury by the merchant, was only a
loan to his future customer, which is now repaid with
compound interest.

The only redeeming virtue in the whole transac-
tion is the fact that a very large portion of the people pay the tax without knowing it. And Shakes-
peare says:—

*"He that is robbed, not knowing he is robbed, is not
robbed at all."*

Be that as it may, the Government manages to get
money enough from the people each year to pay its
most extravagant expenses, and rapidly reduce the
public debt. During the last fiscal year, ending June
30, 1882, about $220,000,000 was raised from taxes
on imports, and $146,000,000 from internal revenue
tax, $366,000,000 per annum. And this vast sum all
comes directly from consumers, nine-tenths of whom
are comparatively poor people.

There are now about ten million voters in the
United States, and this tax, equally divided among
them, would amount to $36.60 each, per annum.
And if each voter was required to pay this large
sum openly each year as a direct poll tax, it would
be denounced by all as a most tyrannical and out-
rageous imposition.

But this is by no means the worst feature of our
revenue system. It causes even a much larger
amount to be paid by the people each year, directly
into the hands of wealthy manufacturing companies
or corporations.

If we take a look into the workings of our revenue
laws in the cotton manufacturing business, we will
find that, according to the last census, we have 756
cotton manufactories in the United States. The
amount of capital invested is, in round numbers,
$208,000,000. The number of operatives employed
is 172,544, of which 97,752 are women and
girls. Added to this are 2,115 officers and clerks.
The whole amount of wages paid during the last
census year was $42,040,510, averaging about $20.00
per month to each individual employed, the officers
and clerks getting the highest wages, as a matter
of course, and the women and girls the least. The
profits of the owners amounted to a little over $63,-
000,000, or about 33 per cent per annum, on the capital invested.

If we purchase a bill of manufactured cotton goods
directly from any of these manufacturers, about one-
third of the purchase money goes directly into the
pockets of the capitalists, while the remaining two-
thirds go to pay for material and labor. We have
to pay at least twenty-five per cent more for the
goods than we ought to pay. All except about eight
per cent, which would be a fair compensation for the
use of the money invested, is directly chargeable to
the tariff.

Had we time and space to examine into the operations of woolen and iron manufactories, the general
results would no doubt be about the same, the
owners making an immense profit, and the operatives
barely a living, with the dread assurance of being
thrown out of employment whenever the business is
overdone, or becomes slack from any other cause.

That a general reduction of the tax on imports
would cause any material reduction in the price of
labor, we do not believe. But it would make an es-
sential difference in the cost of living, as we will
show more clearly by the following extract from a

speech of Senator Maxey, of Texas, as published in the *Vidette*, a periodical published at Washington City:—

"The farmer whose whole mind is bent on his agricultural pursuits, has neither the time nor opportunity to investigate the influence of the tariff tax on his household expenses. It is a fact, however, that every article he uses is either directly subject to a tariff tax, or its price is enhanced by the tariff. Let us enumerate these burdens. The farmer in the West, where lumber is scarce, pays either a direct or enhanced tax of 20 per cent on the lumber his house is built of; a tax of 35 per cent on the paint it is painted with; of 90 per cent on the window glass; of 35 per cent on the nails; of 53 per cent on the screws; of 30 per cent on the door-locks; of from 35 to 40 per cent on the hinges; of 35 per cent on the wall paper; of from 60 to 70 per cent on his carpets; of 40 per cent on his crockery; of 38 per cent on his iron hollow ware; of 35 per cent on his cutlery; of 40 per cent on his glassware; of from 35 to 40 per cent on the linen he uses in his household; of 50 per cent on the common Castile soap he uses; and 48 per cent on the starch.

"When he goes into his barn, stable, or workshop, he will find that he pays 35 per cent on the iron he uses; 53 per cent on halter chains; 45 per cent on the files or rasps he may use; 47 per cent on the buck saw; 49 per cent on the cross-cut saw; 38 per cent on the hand saw; and 35 per cent on any sheet iron he may require. On his medicines he pays from 20 to 40 per cent; and on his sugar he pays a tax of at least 60 per cent. And as for the clothing he and his family use, let us enumerate the tax separately. On his wool hat he pays from 60 to 80 per cent; on his fur hat, from 45 to 60 per cent; on his suit of woolen clothes, some 55 per cent; on the leather for his boots and shoes, 35 per cent; on his hosiery, 35 per cent. On his wife's and daughter's common alpaca dress, he pays from 65 to 70 per cent; on spool thread, 70 per cent; and on needles, 35 per cent.

"If we were inclined to follow these topics further, it would take up too much time; suffice it to say that the furnishing of his child's cradle, and the coffin in which he is finally buried, pay either a direct tax, or are enhanced in price by our tariff system."

Our internal revenue system, in its operations, is no improvement upon our tariff or imports. Upon careful investigation the showing is, if possible, even much worse.

Of the immense sums raised each year by the general Government from this source, by far the greater portion is derived from the heavy tax on whisky and tobacco. It is generally understood that Congress imposed this burdensome tax upon these two articles upon the hypothesis that they are harmful luxuries, and by no means necessaries of life, and could therefore be easily dispensed with by all who found the tax too burdensome.

This would no doubt be very good logic were the principal consumers the only ones who suffer; but such is not the case. The consumers are mostly grown men, and generally very poor men at that, while the principal sufferers are innocent and helpless women and children. An inordinate use of intoxicating beverages and of tobacco, has always been an oppressive burden upon the community at large, even when untaxed, and their price very little above the cost of production and manufacture, and it may have been intended that this tax should cause a reduction in their consumption; but such has not been the case. Acquired tastes and habits have proved stronger than the love of money, home, or family.

Some of us can remember when small distilleries were scattered all over most of the States, and pure whisky was everywhere sold at from twenty cents to thirty cents per gallon, and any ordinary poor man could get as drunk as a lord, for less than a quarter of a dollar. But since the tax of ninety cents per gallon has been levied upon it by the general Government, and each State and county have added an additional tax or license, a grand era of speculation in whisky has ensued. Large companies have been organized, and mammoth distilleries erected, and the business has assumed most gigantic proportions. Armies of agents in the employ of these great companies swarm over the country, traveling in elegant style, and spending money in the most extravagant profusion. They search for customers in every nook and corner of the Union, and set the example of extravagant debauchery, by drinking copiously themselves, and inviting all whom they chance to meet to drink with them at their expense.

The legitimate consequences of all this speculation and excitement have been to increase the demand and raise the price of whisky to a very high figure. In fact, very little pure whisky can now be had, except from first hands, at any price. The temptation to adulterate it on account of the taxes upon it, and its greatly enhanced price, is so great that very little indeed ever passes through the hands of any ordinary retail dealer, and many of them could safely swear that there is not a drop of pure whisky in the villainous concoctions which they every day sell as such to their deluded customers. And yet each dealer is required to have a license, or, in other words, a certificate of copartnership, posted in some conspicuous place behind his bar, to show that the Government is a partner with him in this vile traffic, and receives a share of the profits.

It has been said that "ours is a Government of the people, by the people, and for the people." If such be the case, each and all of us have the distinguished

honor of being accomplices in this low, base robbery
of the poor, who receive a thousand times worse
than nothing in exchange for the money taken from
them.   We have every day taken the last dime from
those who are worse than widowed mothers, and
stolen the bread from the mouths of their children.
And millions on millions of this ill-gotten gain are
every year poured into the plethoric coffers of the
rich.

*"But from him that hath not shall be taken away
even that which he hath"* not.

It would seem that in a popular Government like
ours, the laborer, the producer, and the tradesman
should have at least a fair and equal share in the great
race of life; but such has not been the case.   For
many years the great tendency of legislation has
been to constantly take from the poor and give to
the rich, making the poor poorer and the rich richer.
But, as we have truly and faithfully endeavored to
show, the letter and spirit of the prophecy of the
text is now. fully and completely fulfilled, and the
hour for a change draws near.   Are capitalists prepared for this change?   By the aid and co-operation
of the Government, they are mounted on very high
horses, and ride rough-shod over the great mass of
the American people.

It is the plain duty of congressmen to enact laws
to restrain the rich and powerful, and aid and encourage the industrious and deserving poor, and to
set an example worthy of being followed by their
constituents.   But their conduct has generally been
quite the reverse.   They have permitted the paid
agents of the banks, the railroads, the manufactories,
and the whisky rings, who are always clamorous for
a fresh pull at the national treasury, to besiege and
infest the halls of Congress during each day, and the
nights are made hideous by the sound of lascivious
and drunken revelry.   And our national capital,

which bears the sacred name of Washington, to the everlasting shame and disgrace of the whole American nation, has gradually become a paradise of harlots, and a den of thieves.

Comrades and brethren, it is your votes and mine which have done all these things. If we continue to elect men to office who are entirely unfit for the business with which they are intrusted, we richly deserve to suffer all the poverty, shame, and disgrace which are the legitimate consequences of our own acts.

In conclusion, would it not be well for some of the wiser heads in Congress to set about devising some scheme for raising money to pay the current expenses of the Government and the public debt, other than by tariff, and internal revenue tax. The time may soon come when the great mass of the people will learn that they are being robbed, and it will be well if Congress and the people at large are not altogether unprepared for that event. Governments are instituted among men to protect life and property, and why should not property be made to bear a just and reasonable share of the expenses of Government?

At all events, it will be well that no more of the public moneys, bonds, lands, or other valuable considerations, should be donated to banking, railroad, steamship, or other rich and powerful corporations, without first submitting the same to a direct vote of the people, to whom the public money and other property actually belong.

If this property belonged to congressmen, they would not be as liberal as they now are in voting it away, and the simple fact of their voting away that which does not belong to them creates a reasonable suspicion, at least, that they profit largely by the operation.

We will now close with the following verses:—

> Most congressmen work half their time
>   On schemes to rob the State;
> The other half each other's crimes
>   They do investigate.
>
> To him that hath, more shall be given,
>   This rule they do obey;
> He that hath nothing under heaven,
>   From him they take away.
>
> They rob the poor to give the rich.
>   Thus millionaires are made.
> The poor may starve in the last ditch,
>   But bankers must be paid.

————o————

IRELAND.

> OH, Ireland, thou land of song,
>   Home of the storied brave,
> Old England cannot very long
>   Thy warlike sons enslave.
>
> The robber must give up the spoil,
>   Too long withheld from thee,
> Give back to Ireland her soil,
>   And make her children free.

A NEW NATIONAL SONG.

THE GODDESS OF LIBERTY.

A VOICE resounds in thunder tone,
Which shakes the earth from zone to zone:
" Who guards the Goddess Liberty
From rebel hordes and tyranny?"
 Millions of freemen shall report,
 And swear with her to hold the fort.
Our fathers hear us from the sky;
We swear to hold the fort or die.

The work our fathers have begun
Is handed down from "sire to son."
No matter who the foe may be,
We draw the sword for Liberty.
 Millions of freemen, &c.

If fierce rebellion should again
Destroy her peace or give her pain,
Or rulers of some foreign State
Their obligations violate,
 Millions of freemen, &c.

She fears not war, though she loves peace,
Which does her wealth and power increase;
But when a foe her peace does mar,
She quickly dons the garb of war.
 Millions of freemen, &c.

Should foreign nations all unite,
And challenge her to deadly fight,
And down the gage of battle throw,
Or at her bosom aim a blow,
 Millions of freemen, &c.

Tyrants shall tremble, kingdoms fall;
Our Union shall survive them all;
Brave hearts shall bleed for Liberty,
The gentle ruler of the free.
 Millions of freemen, &c.

Her starry flag shall be unfurled
By every State throughout the world;
Then Peace shall sit at her right hand,
And war no more shall curse the land.
  Millions of freemen, &c.

Long may our gentle goddess live,
And all mankind true homage give,
The world one grand republic be,
Its watchword, God and Liberty.
  All nations shall to her report,
  And swear with her to hold the fort.
The echo rolls along the sky,
We swear to hold the fort, or die.

GRAND ARMY OF LABOR.

IT is the principal object and design of this Association to elect State and national legislators who will make it their business to incorporate into the laws of the country the principles and purposes contained in the following platform, and judicial and executive officers who will properly interpret and enforce them.

PLATFORM.

First—We demand that the United States revenue and banking laws, which annually cause many millions of dollars to be taken from the poor and given to the rich, should be substantially modified or repealed.

Second—We demand that all steamship, railroad, and telegraph lines should be placed under the direct supervision and control of the general Government.

Third—We demand a safe, reliable, and truly national circulating medium of exchange, without the intervention of banks, and which shall be kept at par with gold and silver coin.

Fourth—We demand that the remnant of the public lands shall be reserved for the inheritance of the people who may actually settle and live thereon, and that all persons who now own or may hereafter own or possess more than one section of land, shall by law be made to pay an extra tax thereon, as an inducement for them to sell a portion to others who are in need of land for homes and cultivation.

Fifth—We demand that a graded tax, the proceeds of which may be applied to the support of the general Government, and payment of the national debt, shall be levied upon all great capitalists and millionaires, as follows:—

Each individual who shall be found to own or possess money, stocks, bonds, and other property to the amount of $100,000 or over, and less than $1,000,000, after deducting all solvent debts, shall be required by law to pay a tax of 1 per cent per annum upon the same into the national treasury. The possessor of $1,000,000 or over, and less than $10,000,000, 2 per cent; $10,000,000 or over, and less than $100,000-000, 3 per cent, and over $100,000,000, 4 per cent.

Sixth—We demand that all incorporated companies shall be required by law: (1) To pay fair and reasonable wages to all of their employes, at stated periods, in cash; (2) The owners or stockholders shall then receive a fair and reasonable rate of interest on the money actually invested in the business; and (3) The net profits shall be equally and fairly divided among stockholders and employes, share and share alike.

Seventh—We demand that the hours of labor be reduced to eight per day, so that laborers may have more time for intellectual improvement and social enjoyment, and be able to reap the advantages conferred by labor-saving machinery, which their own brains have created.

Eighth—We demand that the Government shall always insure an abundance of work for all who necessarily have to depend upon their own labor for subsistence; and guarantee sufficient pay for their services to supply them with food, clothing, shelter, and fuel sufficient to make them comfortable.

Ninth—We demand the prohibition of the employment of children under fourteen years of age in workshops, mines, and factories.

Tenth—We demand the enactment of laws to secure to both sexes equal pay for equal work.

Eleventh—We demand that when a citizen of the United States can be proved, beyond a doubt, to have sold his vote at any election for any consideration or price whatever, laws enacted for that purpose shall make the sale perpetual, and he shall in this manner, by his own act, be disfranchised for life.

Twelfth—We demand laws to punish theft, somewhere in proportion to the amount stolen, and not the reverse, as now generally practiced in our courts.

Thirteenth—We demand the enactment of laws that shall give mechanics and laborers a first lien on their work for their full pay, and the necessary expenses of foreclosing said lien.

Fourteenth—And, finally, we demand equal civil and political rights for all citizens, without regard to sex.

This platform has a solid, bedrock foundation. But if, upon trial, any plank should prove unsound it may be removed, and a new one put down in its place. It may also be extended by adding new planks, until there is standing room for all the industrial classes of the country, which now comprise about nine-tenths of the population.

ADDRESS TO WORKINGMEN.

A NEW POLITICAL ORGANIZATION RECOMMENDED.

COMRADES: In this free and enlightened country and age, the industrial classes really have the power in their own hands, and can, and of right ought to, control and shape the destinies of the nation and the world.

Without labor there would be no wealth, no prosperity, and no happiness. The world would be a barren and dreary waste, devoid of all that makes life desirable or even possible, except to a very limited extent, and under the most miserable circumstances.

But the labor of no one man, in any particular section of the world, can produce all that is necessary for his comfort and happiness. Hence the necessity of merchants or traders to exchange the raw material for the manufactured articles required for commerce, and the products of one country for those of another; so that each individual, live where he may, can have and enjoy the fruits and productions of all the climates and countries of the world.

To facilitate trade, ships, railroads, and canals have been found necessary and convenient. These should all be constructed, managed, and owned by the Government, and used for the common benefit of all the people.

But it is not always convenient or desirable to exchange one product or article of merchandise directly for another, and for that reason a medium of exchange has been invented, usually called capital or

money. Men who have managed to accumulate a
large amount of this medium of exchange, are usually called capitalists or bankers.

Without this medium of exchange millionaires
would not be possible, as the natural and manufactured products of the earth are too bulky and perish-
able to be held in such vast quantities as money and
stocks.

Capital, though really of much less consequence
than trade or labor, has somehow managed to get the
control of both; and capitalists, though claiming to
be a great benefit to society, sometimes prove to be
an irreparable injury and curse by hoarding up and
withholding the money required for general circulation, and also by corrupting legislation and the
courts, and attempting to control them for their own
vile and selfish purposes, to the great injury of the
people and the shame of the Government.

Accumulated capital can easily be dispensed with
without any serious injury to society or the State;
but trade and labor are an absolute necessity, and
should be protected, fostered, and encouraged by
every means within the power of the Government.

What, then, is capital that it should demand and
receive all the profits of labor, enterprise, and skill?
Or why should not labor demand and receive a just
and reasonable share of its own hard-earned productions? Why should the toiling millions cringe like
galley slaves in the presence of capital, and accept a
mere pittance for their valuable services, barely
enough to prolong a miserable existence, to be spent
in the service of capital, piling up its millions?

The wealth of the country is fast passing into the
hands of the few at the expense of the many. At
one extreme, millionaires are accumulating wealth
and increasing in numbers with the most astonishing
rapidity, and at the other, tramps and paupers are
increasing a thousand-fold faster. If this state of
7

things is to continue a few years longer, the charter of our liberty will not be worth the parchment upon which it is written.

We may well arouse ourselves from our Rip Van Winkle sleep of twenty years, and ask each other, What is the cause of all this, and in what manner can we interpose to ward off so dire a calamity, and once more snatch the free institutions of our country from impending ruin?

The answer is very plain and simple, indeed. For these many years we have been sending men to Congress who are either monopolists themselves or directly in the service of monopolists, and receiving higher pay from them than they do from the Government; and it is the most natural thing in the world that they should serve those best who pay them best.

In other words, a very large proportion of the ablest and most prominent members of both houses of Congress are lawyers, who are directly in the employment and under the pay of the great banking, railroad, or manufacturing corporations of the country, from which they receive much larger salaries or fees each year than they do from the general Government. Consequently, when matters in the interest of any of these corporations are brought before Congress, it is not strange, in the least degree, that these hired and salaried representatives of monopoly should be on the alert, and always ready to advocate the cause and interests of their masters with tireless energy and zeal.

But any subject or matter in the interests of trade or labor fails to arouse in them the least degree of enthusiasm, and each of these learned and wise statesmen seems all at once to be completely enveloped in a mantle of the most impenetrable darkness, ignorance, and doubt.

A very large proportion of our congressmen seem to have come to the sage conclusion that a working-man has no rights that a capitalist is bound to respect, and, in consequence, it has now become their principal occupation and business to enact laws which have a direct tendency to make the rich richer and the poor poorer.

For example: Our revenue system is a wonderfully brilliant and complete system for robbing the poor. Our banking system is a no less brilliant system for donating to the rich. Our railroad system is another pet child of Congress, upon which has been lavished all the fond endearments that wealth could bestow or station command. It has constantly been fostered and nursed with such care that it has already grown almost beyond the control of its progenitors. For it the bread has been stolen from the mouths of the children of the people, and their inheritance taken away from them by force of the strong arm of the Government.

Let us recapitulate, and let facts be produced to explain and strengthen our position. Congress has, through its tariff and internal revenue laws, levied a burdensome tax upon nearly every manufactured article of merchandise necessarily consumed by the people. This tax has the effect to limit importation and bar out competition, and of course enhances the price of each article the full amount of the tax, so that the home manufacturer, by cutting down the wages of his employes to the lowest possible figure, is often able to realize as high as 100 per cent upon the capital actually invested, over and above all expenses for material and labor. Congress, by its banking laws, gives each United States banking company 90 per cent of its capital in United States bank notes as a circulating medium, and pays these bonds over twenty million dollars interest each year on United States bonds, held in trust by the Government as security for these notes. By this arrangement bankers are enabled to realize about four times the usual interest on the property or money actually owned by them.

But for all these favors the Government receives comparatively nothing from bankers in return.

Congress has, through its railroad laws, donated a very large amount of Government bonds and nearly two hundred million acres of the public lands, and the right of way everywhere over private as well as public lands, besides many other benefits and privileges to rich and powerful railroad corporations, which endow them with an inheritance and power that kings might envy—for all of which the Government receives very little or nothing in return.

When we consider the rate at which the wealth of the whole country is being absorbed by these great corporations, we are struck with wonder and amazement at the short-sightedness of our congressmen, or, what is more likely, their criminal neglect of duty towards the whole people of these United States. And we are still more surprised at the comparative silence and inactivity of the great mass of the people, who are quietly permitting their liberties and the vast inheritance given them by their forefathers to so easily slip from their grasp. There is a remedy for these evils which is within the reach of every American citizen. We must appeal to the ballot-box. But we cannot depend upon either of the old political organizations. In them there is no longer room for hope. They are sold beyond redemption to the powers of monopoly, and the deeds of their sale are recorded in the *Congressional Records* at Washington.

The famous old Democratic party, which had furnished so many noble Presidents to the country, and governed it with honor and credit for a long series of years, yielded at last to the persuasive eloquence of the slave power, and stepping down from its high position in the confidence of the people, declared its readiness to sacrifice the liberties of the country upon the altar of slavery, and deluged the fairest portion of our land with the blood of the people.

The great Republican party, after having performed its Herculean task of subduing the rebellion, destroying slavery, and restoring the Union, seems to have become intoxicated with success and power, and to have permitted itself to be captured in turn by the powers of monopoly. Its leaders have fallen down before the great money kings of the North, and bent the suppliant knee to the god of mammon. The tall shadows of the giants of monopoly already cover the land and shut out the cheering rays of the glorious sun of liberty from the great majority of the American people.

On the one hand may be seen the pride and circumstance, the glittering show and luxury, of wealth and power; and on the other hand the misery, distress, and want of the deserving poor, who are often deprived of their only means of subsistence by the one-sided laws and usages of the country. The great mass of the people are becoming more and more restless under the heavy yoke of bondage which is every day pressing harder and harder upon their shoulders. Labor strikes and riots are becoming alarmingly frequent and powerful, but capital lives at its ease while labor is starved into terms. What, then, remains for us to do? The only alternative left us is to unite and form a new political party, with new ideas, new principles, and new leaders—leaders who will seek the greatest good for the greatest number, and who love humanity better than money.

The Knights of Labor is a splendid, well-appointed, and powerful organization in the interests of labor, and, although not itself political in character, it is well calculated to act as pioneer or vanguard to a great political organization, and all other labor associations, of whatever character, should wheel into line and stand shoulder to shoulder in the grand army of labor, whose principal weapons will be the

votes of its soldiers. When this army is once fully
organized and under careful and thorough discipline,
it will be invincible to any force that monopoly can
send against us.

It should ever be the aim of the Grand Army of
Labor to conquer by the ballot alone, although it
should take long years of weary toil and patient for-
bearance. But sad experience has already taught
us that to demand justice without the power to enforce the demand generally amounts to very little or
nothing. And if our oppressors should continue in
the future, as in the past, to defeat our peaceful efforts
to obtain justice, by using the abundant means within
their control in corrupting and intimidating voters,
legislators, and courts; and, above all, if they continue to employ detectives to ensnare, and armed
soldiers to shoot down and bayonet unsuspecting
and defenseless crowds of famishing men, women,
and children, simply because they meet to petition
and remonstrate against those who have robbed
them of their earnings and then turned them out-of-
doors to starve and perish with cold, then forbear-
ance may cease to be a virtue, and we may be compelled to meet force with force. And, if that time
ever should come—which may God forbid—it will be
well for us not to be entirely unprepared for the
mighty contest.

Self-preservation is nature's first and greatest law,
and it cannot be expected that men, who in childhood were rocked in the cradle of liberty and who
have the warm blood of revolutionary sires still
coursing through their veins, should readily become
the willing slaves of corporate tyranny and greed.

It has hitherto been our proud boast that ours was
a Government of the people, by the people, and for
the people. But it has become a Government of corporations, by corporations, and for corporations; and
our boasted

"Land of the free and home of the brave"

Is fast becoming a nation of millionaires and tramps.

There was doubtless a great oversight in the formation of the Constitution of the United States in not limiting the amount of land and other property that an individual or corporation might own or possess.

We do not object to giving any man the free privilege of accumulating wealth to any reasonable amount, so that he may be able to spend his declining years in ease and comfort. In fact, we respect and honor the man who, by his industry and frugality, has been able to provide for himself a home and plenty of means for the support of himself and all who are dependent upon him, and we believe that he should be protected in his right and peaceable possession of this property by the laws of the country and the whole force of the Government.

But there should be somewhere a limit to a man's accumulations. No one man, or even a corporation, should be permitted to own the whole world, nor a continent, nor even a State. All wealth comes through labor and the free gift of an all-wise Providence, and is intended for the common good of all his creatures. No man should for an instant be deprived of the right to labor, or of a reasonable share of the product of his labor, or, in other words, of the wealth his labor creates. No man, because he is more powerful than another, should be permitted to take the product of his labor or means of subsistence and place it beyond his reach or absorb it as a part of his own possessions. Nor should any combination of men be permitted to thus rob their fellows for the purpose of accumulating vast estates for which they have no earthly use.

Any State whose constitution and laws permit an unlimited accumulation of wealth in the hands of the few, bears in its bosom the seeds of its own dissolution and decay. We can already name three or four men

whose united wealth would place them entirely beyond
the reach of law and government, while thousands of
other men, women, and children are actually suffering and dying for want of a small portion of that
wealth which properly belongs to them and which
has been created by their own labor. Hence, we
claim that all individuals and corporations which
have accumulated more than sufficient wealth to
place them beyond the reach of want should be sub-
jected to a graded tax for the support of the Government, which would have the effect to check them
in their mad career and remove a part of the burden
of taxation from the shoulders of those who are less
able to bear it. Such a thing as equal and uniform
taxation does not and cannot exist. This question
has been fully and forever settled by the courts and
the constitutional conventions of States. And, besides
this, it is a well-known fact that, as a general rule,
men of moderate means pay three or four times the
amount of taxes in proportion to the amount of their
property that is paid by the great corporations and
men of wealth generally.

If a person enters a homestead or preëmption
claim on the public domain, his claim is at once taxed
at the full price of Government lands, besides the
improvements, if any. But the great railroad corporations refuse to pay any tax at all on the many
millions of acres that the Government has too gener-
ously given them. In fact, it has been a very difficult
matter to collect any taxes whatever from some of
these great and powerful corporations. They seem
already above paying taxes and above the reach of
the law. When they do pay anything, they pay
about what they please and when they please. But
a poor man who neglects to pay his taxes is at once
sold out by the sheriff, and thus relieved of paying
taxes in the future. Bankers do not pay taxes on
the hundreds of millions of Government bonds they

hold; but they are very prompt in collecting the interest on these bonds, and it must be paid in gold, too. Silver is good enough for common people, but these powerful pets of the Government must be paid in gold.

If the introduction and general use of labor-saving machinery would have the effect, as it should, to shorten the hours of labor so as to give all an opportunity whose inclinations or necessities require them to labor, and at the same time wages could be kept at such a figure as would place the workingman beyond the reach of want, then would the world become a paradise indeed. Then no more little children who ought to be at school or on the play ground, would be found in the mills and workshops, dragging out a miserable existence, wasting their sweet young lives and stunting their growth; no more women who should be engaged in domestic duties, in the care of their homes, and in the proud and interesting business of raising young Americans, would be required at the factories. The general health of the people would be improved and their lives lengthened, and they would become more industrious, sober, and intelligent, more fitting to be the proud citizens of a free and happy country. We shall need the ready wit and willing hand of woman to help us solve these great and difficult social and political problems which now crowd so heavily upon us for solution. She is in the endearing and threefold relations of sister, wife, and mother, the genial partner of our homes and of all our joys and sorrows; why not our partner in the ballot in which she ought to be equally interested with ourselves? She has proved herself our equal in intelligence and judgment, and more than our equal in all that relates to true piety, social refinement, and moral worth. Why, then, should she not have an equal voice in the selection of our rulers and in shaping the destinies of our common country?

A Government which cannot so order its affairs that all its citizens can be provided with business or labor at a remuneration which will furnish food, clothing, shelter, and fuel sufficient for comfort, and still leave plenty of time for rest, study, and amusement, may be set down as a failure.

But we should not attempt to cast all the blame of the shortcomings of the Government upon the shoulders of the rich, nor upon those who, at present, have the management and control of the Government. The fault is in a great measure our own. When our great prototype, the republic of Rome, was on the down grade to ruin on account of her lands and other property having been concentrated in the hands of the few; while the great mass of the people were little better than slaves, clamoring against their Government and to high Heaven for their daily bread, Casius, the great conspirator, is wont to say, "*The fault is not in the gods, but in ourselves that we are underlings.*" If such, indeed, was the case under a Government where the great mass of the people were kept in a state of the most profound ignorance and superstition, and where they had little or no voice in the choice of their rulers, or influence in shaping the destinies of their country, how much more is it our fault, who are blessed with free schools and have the privilege of choosing nearly all the officers of our Government. The Government of Washington and Jefferson, which has been handed down to us by our forefathers, with its free schools, free press, and free ballot, is indeed the noblest and best Government that does now or ever did exist in this world; and if we are so base and cowardly as to fail to maintain it in its integrity, and transmit it unsullied to posterity, we deserve to be slaves.

Any man claiming to be an American, who is so devoid of patriotism, so lost to all sense of honor and shame, as to sell his vote, for any consideration, is entirely unworthy the proud title of American citizen, and should be disfranchised forever.

Nearly all the evils that now seem to thicken around us and threaten us on every side can be remedied by a careful and proper use of the ballot, and without any necessary disturbance of the public peace and prosperity. If there are any provisions in 'the constitutions of our States or nation that stand in the way of our liberties, they can be altered or amended. If laws are enacted which are calculated to do us an injustice or deprive us of any of our rights, they may be repealed and better laws enacted in their stead. If by any chance men are elected to office who prove themselves unworthy our confidence and esteem, we must drop them forever, and be careful in the future to elect better men. Any man who gets himself elected to office as a member of Congress or the Legislature of any State for the vile purpose of selling his vote and influence to the highest bidder, should, like a poisonous serpent, be crushed beneath the heel of every true American citizen.

The principal source of corruption in the two old political parties originates in the primary elections. In these the better class of citizens seem to take very little or no interest, and seldom honor them with their presence; consequently the professional politician and his backer, the monopolist, have full play, and the judicious use of a little money goes a long way towards electing such delegates to the various conventions as will nominate the tools of monopoly to the various offices in the gift of the people; and when their names have once been placed on the ticket by a party convention, a little more money and the party lash is used to insure their election. The monopolist does not care which party the candidate belongs to. The only requirement is that he should serve his master faithfully.

The only remedy for all the evils herein enumerated is for the people to unite, organize, and pull together. The Grand Army of Labor has been devised and instituted for that purpose. It is intended that at least one branch of this united and powerful organization should be established in every precinct in each State of the Union, and each congressional district is to be placed in charge of a district marshal, whose business it will be to organize new branches and attend to the discipline and order of all the branches within his district.

These several branches of the Grand Army of Labor are expected to elect their own delegates, hold their own conventions, nominate their own candidates, *and elect them.* And then if any of the officers of the Government so elected should prove untrue to their trust, justice will be meted out to them with the whole force of a united and powerful organization. In conclusion, the whole matter at issue is concentrated in one single word, and that word is, *organize.*

PREAMBLE AND CONSTITUTION.

WHEREAS, both of the old political parties have been captured, and securely bound, hand and foot, by the great banking, railroad, and manufacturing corporations of the country, who have formed powerful combinations among themselves, and with each other, against the most vital and indispensable rights and interests of trade and labor (the only sure and sound foundation of our national wealth, prosperity, and happiness), and thereby threaten to overthrow and destroy the most sacred rights and liberties of the people of these United States, it has therefore become the highest and most solemn duty of each and all of us, who love liberty and the free institutions of our country, and truly represent the sacred rights and interests of trade and labor, to cast off all allegiance to each of the old political parties, and promptly unite in forming a new political organization, by adopting, and pledging our lives and sacred honor to support, the following

CONSTITUTION.

ARTICLE I.

NAME AND CHARACTER.

This organization shall be known as the Grand Army of Labor, and shall be threefold in character, viz.: Social, Political, and Military; and its motto, Liberty, Unity, and Equality.

ARTICLE II.

ITS BRANCHES.

Branches of the general organization shall be speedily and firmly established in every possible locality, in each and every congressional district throughout the whole country, each of which shall be designated and numbered as follows: Branch No. —, — District, State of ——.

ARTICLE III.

DUTIES OF BRANCHES.

Each branch shall meet at regular, stated periods, to elect its own officers, to receive new members, to discuss and vote upon all questions of interest which may properly be brought before it, and to elect delegates to all county and district conventions. The regular official terms of the officers of each branch shall be one year, or until their successors are elected and qualified.

ARTICLE IV.

CONVENTIONS.

Conventions shall be held in each congressional district, at least once in every two years, to nominate candidates for Congress, to elect district marshals, and delegates to all State and national conventions.

SECTION 2. County and State conventions shall be held as often, at least, as it shall be necessary to nominate county and State officers.

SEC. 3. National conventions shall be held at least once every four years, to nominate candidates for President and Vice-President of the United States; to amend or revise the constitution and general regulations of this organization, when necessary and proper; to elect a marshal general; to make public declarations of its plans and principles, and to transact other necessary and important business for the public good.

ARTICLE V.

MARSHALS.

District and State marshals, and also one marshal-general for the United States, shall be elected by the district State and national conventions, respectively, each of whom shall appoint as many deputies as may be necessary for the labor required to be done.

SECTION 2. It shall be the duty of each district marshal to organize new branches, supervise the discipline of all the branches in his district, and install their officers. He shall also act as temporary chairman at the organization of each district convention, and shall make a quarterly report to tne State marshal, giving a full and comprehensive account of his operations and success, with the whole number of branches in his district, and also the numerical strength of each branch. He shall hold his office during a term of two years, unless he shall sooner become disqualified, in which case his first deputy shall perform his duties.

SEC. 3. The State marshal-general shall call all district and State conventions; establish new districts in his State, preside as temporary chairman at each State convention, and receive, condense, and transmit all official reports from the district marshals in his State to the marshal-general. His regular official term shall be three years.

SEC. 4. The marshal-general shall be the acknowledged head of the organization, and shall serve during a term of four years, unless sooner disqualified. He shall take great care that the organization may be firmly established in every State and Territory of the Union, and that its officers perform their respective duties. He shall issue all necessary proclamations calling conventions, etc.; publish quarterly reports in relation to the progress and strength of the organization in each State, and make such recommendations as he, in his wisdom, shall deem necessary and proper. He shall also preside as temporary chairman at the organization of each national convention, and transact all other business coming within his line of official duty.

ARTICLE VI.

Trade or labor clubs, of whatever name and character, shall be permitted (and they are hereby respectfully requested) to send delegates to all Grand Army of Labor Conventions, upon the same terms as other branches of the organization.

ARTICLE VII.

This organization, upon assuming its military character, shall be guided and governed by the most approved " manual of arms," and the United States Articles of War. For purposes of drill, parade, or actual service, the marshal-general shall assume the title and perform the duties of a major-general of volunteer militia; each grand State marshal, that of a brigadier-general, and each district marshal, that of a colonel, and their deputies shall act as staff officers. All the officers of each branch shall assume the titles and duties of officers of a military company, in regular order and rotation, from captain down to the eighth corporal. The district marshal, when ordered by his superior officers, shall designate some officer who is well acquainted with military tactics, to act as drill master of each branch in his district.

ARTICLE VIII.

FREEDOM OF SPEECH AND ACTION.

Nothing in this constitution shall require any person to perform military duty contrary to his own individual interests, or inclinations. Nor shall any member be censured or blamed for any opinion or vote he may give contrary to the supposed interests of this organization, unless it can be made to appear that he has been unduly influenced, or bribed, or is otherwise working in the interests and pay of the enemy.

ARTICLE IX.

TRIALS AND PUNISHMENTS.

In case that any member shall knowingly, and willfully, violate this constitution, or any of the laws or regulations of this organization, or shall in any way conduct himself in a disorderly or improper manner, any member may bring specific charges against him, which shall be presented to the proper officers of the branch of which he is a member, and upon such presentation, a committee of competent and impartial members shall be appointed to try the case, and present the testimony taken, in writing, to the branch, which shall take a vote upon it at the next regular meeting, to determine the guilt or innocence of the accused. And in case a majority of the members present find him guilty, he may be fined, reprimanded, or expelled, as the chief officer of the branch shall deem proper. Any officer of this organization may, in the same manner, be tried and impeached for bad conduct, or any misdemeanor in office, by any convention properly having jurisdiction in his case.

ARTICLE X.

No millionaire, banker, usurer, railroad manager, stock broker, corporation, lawyer, Chinaman, or any other person who is known, for any cause whatever, to be opposed to the principles, objects, and purposes of this association, shall ever become, or remain a member thereof. But all workingmen, mechanics, tradesmen, operatives, producers, merchants, and all other persons who have arrived at the age of eighteen years, who are opposed to monopoly and oppression,

8

and who are willing to cast their lot with us, and aid us with their counsels, their influence, and their votes, shall be eligible to membership.

ARTICLE XI.

SECTION 1. The meetings and general business of each branch of this association shall be more or less secret, as may be deemed necessary for its welfare and preservation.

SEC. 2. At any particular meeting of a branch under favorable circumstances, and when there is no business of a private nature to be transacted, a limited number of invitation cards, signed by the N. C.'s and N. V. C.'s, and countersigned by the N. R.'s, may be issued to parties (not members) who are known to be friendly to the cause, but in no other manner shall visitors who are not members be admitted.

SEC. 3. Members of other branches may at any time be admitted by card, signed by the chief officers of the branches to which they belong.

SEC. 4. When public lectures for the benefit of the association are given, the officers and members may appear in uniform, and occupy their regular places in the hall; but on such occasions no other business, except that pertaining to the lecture, shall be transacted.

ARTICLE XII.

Money to defray the necessary expenses of this association may be raised by subscription, lectures, or social parties, but no regular system of weekly or monthly dues shall ever be established.

ARTICLE XIII.

AMENDMENTS.

This constitution and the general regulations for branches, shall not be revised, altered, or amended, except by a national convention, and a majority vote of two-thirds of all the branches.

GENERAL REGULATIONS.

ARTICLE 1.

EACH and every branch of this association shall, at the time of its organization, and at its last regular meeting before the 22d day of February of each year, ever after, elect one of each of the following officers, who shall be installed at the next regular meeting, and serve during a term of one year, or, until their successors are duly installed, viz., Noble Chief, Noble Vice-Chief, Noble Recorder, Noble Corresponding Secretary, Noble Financier, Noble Treasurer, Noble Marshal, Noble Vice-Marshal, Noble Guardian, and Noble First, Second, Third, and Fourth Sentinels; and as soon as convenient, after installation, the N. C. shall appoint a Noble Ex-Chief, Worthy Chaplain, Worthy Musician, Worthy Room Warden, and four Pages.

ARTICLE 2.

SECTION 1. It shall be the duty of the N. C. to preside at all meetings of his branch, preserve order, and enforce the laws thereof; send for absent officers or members whenever he or the branch may think it necessary and proper; announce, or cause to be read by the N. R., all questions and resolutions before the branch for discussion; call for the yea and nay, when required by the branch; give the casting vote in case of a tie, and perform all other acts and duties u-ually belonging to a presiding officer.

SEC. 2. The N. V. C. shall have the especial charge of the admission of members and visitors at each regular meeting; supervise and direct the conduct of the N. G. and Sentinel; and, in case of the absence of the N. C., he shall preside in his stead.

Sec. 3. The N. R. shall keep, in a Book of Records, a just and true account of the proceedings of each meeting; read before the branch all resolutions proposed for discussion, when requested by the N. C.; record in a book, kept for that purpose, all resolutions of a public and general character, which have been approved by the branch, and procure the signature of the N. C. thereto, and attest the same with the place and date of approval. He shall read his reports at the commencement of each regular meeting.

Sec. 4. The N. C. S. shall, when requested by the N. C. or the branch, write and transmit all reports, orders, or other official documents, to other branches, or to the superior officers of the organization. He shall also receive, read before the branch, answer, as directed by the branch or N. C., and preserve on file all the correspondence or official documents addressed through him to the branch.

Sec. 5. It shall be the duty of the N. F. to receive or collect all moneys due the branch from its members or other persons, and immediately hand the same over to the N. T., taking his receipt therefor. He shall keep a cash book, in which shall be entered each and every sum received, when and from whom received; and all receipts from the N. T. shall be written on alternate pages, opposite the accounts, and signed by that officer.

Sec. 6. The N. T. shall receive all moneys and other valuables collected by the N. F., and belonging to the branch, and safely keep the same, subject only to warrants or orders drawn on him by the branch, signed by the N. C. and attested by the N. R. He shall also keep a cash book, on opposite pages of which shall be kept a full and complete account of all receipts and disbursements, in such a manner as to enable him to report at the close of each meeting the amount received, the amount expended, and the amount remaining on hand.

Sec. 7. The N. M. shall be master of ceremonies, and shall have a care that all movements of the officers and members of the branch are conducted with proper discipline and decorum; also that the room is kept in order and properly lighted, and that all officers are in their proper places, and that all members and visitors are properly seated, and clothed in appropriate uniform or regalia.

Sec. 8. The N. V. M. shall act under the direction of the N. M. and assist him in the performance of his duties and, in case of his absence, he shall act in his stead.

Sec. 9. The N. G. shall keep the inner door and permit none to enter who do not possess the proper qualifications, except by express command of the N. V. C. or N. C.

Sec. 10. The Noble Sentinels shall guard the outer door, and may relieve each other every half hour, and they shall go to each other's assistance when ordered by the N. V. C. or N. C.

Sec. 11. The N. E. C. shall be chosen from among those who have served as N. C., when any such belong to the branch. He shall have no authority, but occupy an honorable position, and his counsels shall be listened to, and considered with profound respect.

Sec. 12. The W. C. shall be a clergyman, deacon, or other religious person, and may read a short passage of Scripture, at the commencement of each meeting, and, when requested by the N. C., may close with a prayer or a benediction.

Sec. 13. The W. M. shall lead the vocal or instrumental music of the branch, and should always be selected with a view to his proper qualifications for the position.

SEC. 14. The W. R. W. shall have charge of the room and furniture, and keep everything in order and safety. He shall have everything in readiness at least fifteen minutes before the hour of meeting, and subject to the inspection and approval of the N. M.

SEC. 15. The Pages shall occupy a seat in front of the N. C. and may at any time be sent by him in quest of absent officers or members, or upon any other business of the branch outside or inside of the room. They should always be selected from among the youngest and most active of the members.

ARTICLE 3.

*In this association there shall be three Primary Degrees, and for each Primary Degree, there shall be three Secondary Degrees. These Degrees shall not be received by any member in less time than three months from each other.

ARTICLE 4.

SECTION 1. The uniform or regalia of this association shall be a scarf placed over the left shoulder, thence crossing at the right side, and around the waist, and fastened at the left side; the ends, with tassels of red, white, and blue, hanging down as low as the knee.

SEC. 2. The scarf worn by members of the first Primary Degree, shall be red; of the Second, white; of the Third, blue or purple. And to designate each Secondary Degree, a rosette shall be attached to the scarf, commencing at a point where it crosses the left breast, ranging from the heart upward; first, red; second, white; and third, blue.

SEC. 3. The insignia of office shall be a star about three inches in diameter from point to point, attached to the scarf directly over the heart. For the First Primary Degree, the star should be made of brass; for the Second, of silver; and for the Third, of gold.

Each official star shall have an appropriate design emblematic of each office respectively, engraved or impressed upon it.

ARTICLE 5.

When any branch has been in active operation during the full term of one year, no person shall be eligible to the office of N. V. C. or N. R. who has not taken the first three Secondary Degrees; nor to the office of N. C., unless he has taken the said Degrees, and served a full term as N. V. C. or N. R.

ARTICLE 6.

Each and every person on being admitted as a member of any branch of this association, shall pay into the treasury thereof the sum of two dollars; and for each degree when taken, two dollars.

OUR LABOR SYSTEM.

THE labor system of the United States, if founded upon just and true principles, and directed with wisdom and prudent care by the Government, will in time become the sure foundation of great and uninterrupted national prosperity.

The laborer is, and of right ought to be, as great a factor in the government of the country as the capitalist or office-holder; and hence the necessity that he should have a thorough education, and that, in his maturer years, he should not be overburdened with work, and should have an abundance of time and opportunity to glean information from books and papers, so as to thoroughly understand the history of the world, the science of government, the character and importance of our free institutions, and also the necessity of placing good and true men in every position of trust and power.

If it has ever been necessary for laboring men to work ten or twelve hours each day (which I do not believe has ever been the case), the great inventors of the present age, by the improvement, introduction, and use of labor-saving machinery, have obviated that necessity. And laboring men, having done their full share towards making all these improvements, are therefore justly entitled to their full share of the benefits to be derived from their use.

It is not enough that laws should be enacted, having for their object the reduction of the time constituting a lawful day's labor; but laboring men themselves must see that these laws are strictly and impartially enforced, until they shall become the established rule and custom in every section of the country, and in every branch of labor throughout the land, and all that without any very considerable reduction of the rates of pay. And yet we must not lose sight of the fact that the price of labor will always be governed more or less by the universal law of supply and demand, and the sooner this great law is more generally understood and acknowledged, the better it will be for all.

If laboring men were more particular about getting employment where the pay is known to be good, and less so in regard to the amount of their pay, they would, in the end, be the gainers, as they would run less risk of being swindled out of their hard-earned money, and also less likely to be thrown out of employment, and the employer and the employe would alike be mutually benefited.

When a man is out of employment, his expenses are generally much greater than when at work. Hence it is not the man who can command the highest wages, but he who works the most steady, and spends the least, who saves the most money.

No man should, under any circumstances, be required, or submit, to work more than eight hours in the twenty-four, and even that time should be divided into two shifts of four hours each. If the work is continuous, day and night, the men should be divided into three "reliefs," the first "relief" to work from eight o'clock to twelve, the second from twelve to four, and the third from four to eight. Day laborers may work from eight o'clock to twelve, and from two to six. By this plan all may have their regular meals and regular sleep, and plenty of time for study and amusement.

Our labor system has been derived, to a great extent, from the old "feudal system" in England. The conquerors enslaved the original owners of the soil, and compelled them to perform all the labor, while their self-constituted masters derived nearly all the benefits, and great care was taken to get the greatest possible amount of work done for the least possible amount of pay. The laborer was forced to work from daylight until dark for the most scanty means of subsistence, and if sickness or misfortune overtook him he and those dependent upon him for support frequently had to suffer for the bare necessaries of life, while their cruel and almost inhuman oppressors fared sumptuously every day, and reveled in luxury and ease.

The same unjust and tyrannical labor system still exists to a greater or less extent in England, and with some slight modifications has been transmitted to our shores. This system is nearly all wrong. The laborer has the first and strongest claim to the products of his own labor, and all such as seek to evade the stern decree that "man must earn his bread by the sweat of his brow," should be content with what is left after the wants, necessities, and comforts of the laborer and producer have been fully and bountifully supplied.

It is estimated that about seventy per cent of the population of our country are producers. This avocation in all its various branches necessitates a vast amount of hard labor in the sun, and is the most useful as well as the most laborious known to the human race. But it is the sure foundation upon which all other avocations, and every other source of human prosperity and happiness, is built. Remove the producer, and the occupation of the mechanic, the manufacturer, and the merchant would be gone at once; the majority of the human race would at once perish for want of food and clothing, and the remainder relapse into the most abject barbarism. Hence the wisdom and necessity that everything possible should be done to encourage the producer in his arduous labors, and make his task easy as possible.

Many and very important improvements have recently been made in agricultural machinery, and many more improvements are every year being brought into use. Yet laboring men are still required to toil in the hot sun in summer ten, twelve, or even fourteen hours each day for less pay than can be obtained in almost any other avocation. This should not be. The task of the producer can and should be made more easy and agreeable, his hours of daily labor be shortened, his toil made as pleasant as possible, and he (though he may be a stranger and a tramp) should be surrounded with all the endearing comforts and pleasures of a home. A bath and change of clothing should be ready for him at the close of each dusty and hot day's work, and he should also be provided with a clean and comfortable bed, and plenty of books, periodicals, and papers to read during his leisure hours.

Although the proper age of man may be put down at one hundred years, yet a very large proportion fail to reach even one-half that number. Many die comparatively young from habits of intemperance and overwork, and others from intemperance and the want of sufficient manly exercise to keep the system in healthy working order. The latter class seem to have taken firm hold of the fallacious idea that it is the tip-top of human excellence and blessedness to live entirely without labor of any kind, either physical or mental. And these idle, worthless creatures have long tried to monopolize the honored name of ladies and gentlemen, and to set themselves above the laboring classes. Let others think as they may, I can see nothing to prevent a true gentleman from being a laboring man, or a laboring man from being a true gentleman. Soft white hands and fine clothes are no indications of a true gentleman; nor is she who labors to manufacture fine silk, or make fine dresses, less a lady, other things being equal, than she who wears them. Fine clothes and idle habits never yet made a true lady or gentleman, and it would be far better for all if those who call themselves ladies and gentlemen would work more and the laboring classes less, and thus meet each other about half way, on common ground, and work together for the good of all. Capital and labor should be made equal partners, and share alike the profits of their enterprise and toil. By this means our pleasures and comforts would be increased, our health ensured, and our lives prolonged. The liberties and free institutions of our country would be preserved, the greatest good to the greatest number be secured, and the comfort and happiness of all the people of the whole nation be increased and perpetuated through all coming time.

In order to consummate these great and most important purposes, we must make earnest and constant appeals to the powers of association, the press, and the ballot-box.

HOURS OF LABOR.

IF all would work three hours each day,
 We could live well indeed,
And always have the cash to pay
 For everything we need.

If half of us would work six hours,
 We would have plenty then
To keep each idle friend of ours,
 And still have cash to lend.

Eight hours each day is quite enough
 For any man to work;
Ten hours each day is rather tough—
 Most ten-hour men will shirk.

Eight hours to work and eight to sleep,
 Eight to improve the mind—
All who this *golden rule* do keep
 Will health and comfort find.

———o———

OUR EAGLE FLAG.

EMBLEM of liberty and love,
 All hail to thee, old glory!
Thy stars were sent thee from above,
 Thy stripes are from Aurora.

CHORUS.

The eagle bold that soars to heaven,
 And scans the solar powers,
His prowess to our *flag* has given,
 The victory is ours.

When freedom's fight had just begun
 And liberty was young,
The eagle soared o'er Washington,
 And round his banners hung.
　　　The eagle bold, &c.

When slavery reared his hydra head
  And threatened liberty,
Our eagle flag to conquest led,
  Till every slave was free.
            The eagle bold, &c.

But now the giant Polypus
  Of leagued monopoly
Has got his thousand claws on us,
  And we no more are free.
            The eagle bold, &c.

Arise, ye knights of liberty,
  And put your armor on;
If you would once again be free,
  The battle must be won.
            The eagle bold, &c.

Ye men of honor and renown,
  Who can't be bought for gold,
Raze mammon's temple to the ground,
  Like Solomon's of old.
            The eagle bold, &c.

Ye veterans of former wars,
  Who fought for liberty,
Ye brave and war-worn sons of Mars,
  Down with monopoly.
            The eagle bold, &c.

————o————

THE WONDERS OF YOSEMITE.*

'TIS well that all should come and see
    These peerless scenes of boundless worth,
  The wonders of Yosemite,
  The grandest scenery of earth.

In summer lay your cares aside,
  If mental exercise you need;
The book of Nature opens wide,
  And all who choose may freely read.

The mountain air is pure and cool,
  The water-falls are grand and high,
The proud domes rise from crystal pool
  And seem to pierce the azure sky.

———— ————
*Yosemite Valley, 4,050 feet above the sea.

The speckled trout in festive play
  Dart through the limpid water cold;
At sight of man they hide away,
  And thus elude the fisher bold.

———

Come in the morning's lovely dawn
  And take a sail on Mirror Lake,
Before the sun has shone upon,
  Or winds its placid waters shake.

Majestic domes* on either side,
  Their tall forms decked with living green;
Each stands erect with regal pride,
  King of the vale and goddess, queen.

Long may they reign as sovereigns still;
  No wars can their firm footing shake;
The elements obey their will;
  Their photographs adorn the lake.

———

Come close beneath these lofty falls†
  And hear the mammoth grizzly roar;
The sound the human ear appalls
  Like surf upon a rocky shore.

Down, down the crystal waters leap,
  Until they reach about half way;
They dash on precipices steep,
  And mostly beat themselves to spray.

If you are strong and wish to see
  The source from whence these waters leap,
Go get your lunch and come with me,
  While we ascend the mountain steep.

As we toil up the northern wall,
  We pause to view the other side,
Where we behold the Vernal Falls
  And high Nevada's foaming tide.

The river plows beneath our feet;
  Bold Glacier Point is just abreast;
Proud Star King's snow-capped crest we greet,
  And dizzy height of grand Cloud's Rest.

———

*South Dome, 5,000 feet above the valley; North Dome, 3,725 feet above the valley.
†Yosemite Falls, 2,624 feet above the valley.

Mount your good horse and come with me
　　To see Nevada's wondrous falls,
And other scenes so far away
　　'Twill take two days to see them all.

As up the mountain trail we go,
　　We pass the beauteous Vernal Falls*
Before we reach the house of Snow,
　　Where we must be when dinner calls.

We must not pass this lovely place
　　Till down the falls we take a peep.
Swift Merced runs with matchless grace,
　　And o'er the brink she takes a leap

Three hundred feet and fifty more,
　　Down to the boiling caves below.
Her gems she flings from shore to shore,
　　As, plunging headlong, down she goes.

A stairway takes us to the foot,
　　Where we may see the crystal cave,
And get our share of gems, to boot,
　　Fresh from the plunging, surging wave.

———

Nevada† we have reached at last,
　　And stand before the mighty falls;
Merced runs furious and fast,
　　And leaps down from her lofty walls.

Her magic charms are all displayed;
　　We hear the music of her voice;
Her grandeur makes us half afraid;
　　'Mid fear and wonder we are lost.

———

River of Mercy, yet how long
　　Will downward plunge thy restless flood;
How long will sound thy happy song,
　　Sweet Nature's tribute to her God?

A few short years, and they who now
　　Adore thy beauty and thy grace,
Will to the land of spirits go,
　　And other men will take their place.

---

*Vernal Falls, 350 feet high.
†Nevada Falls, 700 feet high.

But thou, ten thousand years or more,
  Will move in thine accustomed place,
And o'er thy granite walls will pour
  Thy crystal floods with youthful grace.

Wise men will come from the far East,
  And scholars from the frozen North
Will lay their honors at thy feet,
  And praise thy beauty and thy worth.

Pilgrims to thee will never cease,
  Of every race, from every shore;
Their numbers will each year increase,
  Till time and tide shall be no more.

Now for the highest peak in sight,*
  From which to take a distant view;
To reach its top requires some might,
  And tries both men and horses, too.

Ten thousand feet and more above
  The ocean's solitary waste;
With modest haste we upward move,
  Until we reach its lofty crest.

A clear, blue sky above our heads,
  Slight, fleecy clouds beneath our feet;
Below we see the valley's bed,
  And far away vast snow-clad peaks.

Mt. Dana looms high in the north;
  Mt. Star King occupies the west;
Beyond a group of minor worth;
  Southeast Mt. Whitney rears his crest.

The last, the loftiest on the coast,
  Full fifteen thousand feet in height,
Should bear a name it well might boast;
  To change it still would be but right.

Brave Clarence King, well known to fame,
  Explored these peaks and took their height;
The highest should have borne his name--
  To do and dare was his delight.

———

Now let us take a pleasant trail
  That leads us down the valley green,
To see the lovely Bridal Veil,†
  By far the fairest falls we've seen.

———

*Cloud's Rest, 6,150 feet above the valley.
†Bridal Veil Falls, 940 feet high.

9

We see the veil, but not the bride,
　　It covers her from head to foot;
Beneath its folds she seems to hide,
　　Nor can we see her wedding suit.

O lovely bride, where is thy groom?
　　Show us the favored, happy man.
Is it the man high in the moon,
　　Or warrior chief El Capitan?

Most charming bride, remove thy veil
　　That we may see thy blushing face,
And gleaming eyes that never fail
　　To flash at thoughts of nuptial bliss. .

Why is it thou art here alone,
　　Chained to the solid granite rock?
Is thy great lover's heart of stone,
　　So hard he will not let thee talk?

Will not thy lover rescue thee
　　From endless bondage and from chains?
Thine ever-faithful friend to be,
　　Where peace and love and honor reigns.

If thou no more wilt show thy face,
　　Or yield' to love's caresses never,
No husband shall thy form embrace.
　　Farewell, sweet bride, farewell forever.

———

To Glacier Point* now let us climb
　　And take the wonders in review,
And Eagle Point, if we have time,
　　But to shun both will never do.

Take a good horse that will not fail
　　As we go up the mountain-side;
We have a winding, zigzag trail,
　　But very good and safe to ride.

Higher and higher we ascend
　　At each succeeding turn we make,
Until we reach the house of Glenn,
　　Where a most welcome lunch we take.

———

*Glacier Point, 3,200 feet above the valley.

Let us approach the mighty wall,
    And take a cautious look below.
Great God ! if we should slip and fall,
    Three thousand feet down we would go.

A girl stepped out upon the rock,
    And stooped to see the fearful sight.
This gave each one a nervous shock,
    And paralyzed her friends with fright.

A lady in the vale below
    Appears no larger than a doll.
Where else on this earth could we go
    To find so high and vast a wall ?

Here we behold Yosemite
    In all her native grace and power;
The water dashing into spray
    Shows lovely rainbows in the shower.

Nevada at a distance, too,
    And lovely Vernal Falls are seen;
Of all the falls in this grand show,
    Nevada is the honored queen.

Some falls we do not even name.
    This is not altogether right,
But as our muse is getting lame
    On falls, we bid them all good-night.

El Capitan* stands forth alone
    Like a brave chieftain in command.
Each crag and cliff his prowess owns,
    And, as a guard, around him stand.

He is the captain of the guard;
    His guardsmen all are on the watch.
His sentinels have duties hard
    As clansmen of the Highland Scotts.

All the great wonders of the vale
    Are objects of his special care;
Likewise each pleasant grove and dale—
    His watchful eye is everywhere.

Now let each resident beware,
    And never do a stranger wrong;
If so, they might as well prepare
    To fall into his clutches strong.

*El Capitan, 3,300 feet above the valley.

Let all be careful what they do,
    And to no vandal deeds resort.
Each tourist he is watching, too,
    And each one's conduct will report.

Ye men of science, can ye tell
    What made these walls so grand and high?
Was it great heat as fierce as h—l
    That caused the earth to open wide?

Did great Jehovah show his wrath
    Through tempest, earthquake, fire, and flood,
Which heaved the mountains, rent the earth,
    'Mid thunder from the throne of God?

Or did the mountains always stand
    Co-equal with the earth itself,
And when soft rocks were washed, as sand,
    Left peaks and valleys, crags, and cliffs?

If falls commenced far down below,
    There were no need of earthquake shocks.
The river by its constant flow
    Would plow a channel through the rocks.

The walls, when soft, would tumble in
    And wash away by rushing tide;
The yielding walls would cave again,
    Thus form a valley deep and wide.

Each year the mountains are less high,
    The mighty ocean bed less deep;
The waters, as they murmur by,
    Their everlasting vigils keep.

Freighted with earth from far above,
    Streams onward to the ocean flow,
And thus each year a share remove,
    The process very sure, yet slow.

The Merced River rushes down
    From mountains clad in robes of snow,
And through the valley hurries on
    To heated plains far down below.

Forever beautiful and clear,
    Except when swelled by snow or rain,
Her softer walls in slopes appear,
    Hard walls as monuments remain.

Some sights far distant we have seen,
  Great fields of never-melting snow;
Grand rapids swift, vast forests green,
  But time is pressing, and we go.

Reclining in Nevada's arms,
  Arrayed in robes of living green,
Yosemite displays her charms,
  With all the grandeur of a queen.

We now are quite prepared to leave
  With abler pens the tale to tell.
O'er their success we will not grieve.
  Scenes of the valley, all farewell.

————o————

THE GREAT REBELLION AND GEN. U. S. GRANT.

WHEN Davis led the South to war,
  And rebel cannon roared,
    On Sumpter Fort, near Charleston Bar,
  Their iron missiles poured.

A message over the wire speeds,
  Well charged with war's alarms,
Which tells the tale of rebel deeds,
  And calls the North to arms.

'Twas thus the spirit of the North
  Was thoroughly aroused.
All party strife was then forgot,
  Likewise domestic vows.

The husband and the lover, too,
  The father and the son,
No more their labors could pursue;
  Each siezed a sword or gun,

And when a call for troops was made
  By our good President,
They rushed to "join the grand parade"—
  To fight was their intent.

So.ne scarce had time to visit home
  To bid their friends good-bye;
Their wives and sweethearts, left alone,
  Were far too brave to cry.

'Twas thus the freemen of the North
  In warlike legions formed.
Armed and equipped they sallied forth,
  Nor cared for sun and storms.

On such their country could rely.
  Their hearts were true and brave;
Though some did for their country die,
  They did their country save.

Their first care was for Washington,
  Our much loved capital,
That it should not by rebel guns
  Or rebel intrigue fall.

While the drilled legions of the East
  Marched down through Baltimore,
The yeomen of the great Northwest
  Sought Mississippi's shore.

These Western men in language true,
  Yet forcible and rough,
Swore they would force a passage through
  From Cairo to the Gulf.

The stars and stripes again should float
  On Mississippi's waves,
And all who dared our flag insult
  Should sleep in rebel graves.

Now for a leader true and bold;
  Though Scott was ever true,
Yet he had grown so very old
  The task he could not do.

McDowell first took the command,
  But he was quite too young.
His troops before the rebels ran
  At the battle of Bull Run.

McClellan next stepped proudly forth
  And took the chief command,
And the brave soldiers of the North
  Thought him the coming man.

He drilled the troops, and did observe
  Their discipline with pride,
And every day, with steady nerve,
  Along the lines did ride.

He thus equipped an "army grand,"
  One hundred thousand strong,
Yet did not long this force command—
  Some thought he suffered wrong.

His orders were: "To Richmond go."
  This called for no reply,
For soldiers have no choice, you know;
  "'Tis theirs to do and die."

At last he marched and met the foe;
  The foe he did defeat,
Yet did not "on to Richmond go,"
  But ordered a retreat.

All this our honest President
  Could scarcely understand.
He asked McClellan to resign,
  And sought another man.

Then Pope and Burnside, Hooker, three,
  Each tried the chief command,
But rebel forces, under Lee,
  Were more than *they* could stand.

Next the command devolved on Meade,
  A man of well-known worth.
Of leaders much we stood in need,
  For Lee was marching North.

Meade met the foe at Gettysburg,
  On Pennsylvania's soil,
And after two days' bloody fight,
  Made him give up his spoils,

And leave the field with fearful waste,
  And hastily march South;
But General Meade was not in haste
  To follow up the route.

While these things happened in the East
  Near the Potomac shore,
The hardy soldiers of the West
  Were moving on with power,

Four mighty armies had been raised,
  And marched on Dixie's soil,
Sometimes advancing in hot haste
  To then again recoil.

Yet one brave chieftain of the West
  Held steady on his course,
And neither turned to right or left
  For any hostile force.

He meant his duty to perform,
  Not heeding rebel rant,
But onward marched through fire and storm.
  This hero's name was Grant.

Fort Henry first he overthrew,
  Then stormed Fort Donaldson,
And on the plains of Shiloh, too,
  A hard-fought battle won.

He then laid siege to Vicksburg Town,
  And captured that stronghold;
Thus swept the Mississippi down
  With Western heroes bold.

He then to Chattanooga went
  To rescue Rosecrans.
The fight that followed that event
  Did freedom's cause advance.

Sherman here took the foe in hand—
  Grant went to Washington.
He was appointed to command
  Our armies all as one.

With Meade as second in command,
  Again Grant took the field
Against the orce of General Lee.
  Now one of two must yield.

The two great captains of the war
  At last must meet in fight;
The contest deepens; *never fear,*
  God will defend the right.

They first met at the Wilderness
  In sanguinary fights.
Their hosts did on each other press
  Three fearful days and nights.

And though the bodies of the slain
  By thousands strewed the field,
Yet neither Grant or Lee could gain,
  Nor any ground would yield.

But Grant then marched around the plain
  To circumvent the foe,
And Lee, before his rear was gained,
  Quite readily did go.   .

The rebels had the hills entrenched
  Along their army's track;
As from their grasp each fort was wrenched,
  To others they fell back.

At Spotsylvania next they met,
  And made the firm hills shake;
A thousand guns with shot and shell
  Each other's ranks did rake.

There is no terror for the brave;
  Each army held its ground,
Till Grant, to further slaughter save,
  Again by flank marched round.

When at Cove Harbor, castled town,
  Again Lee offered fight,
Which lasted from the early dawn
  Until the dead of night.

But Grant here failed to take their works,
  And lost a host of men,
So marched around these warlike Turks
  For Richmond, on again.

Grant to Bermuda Hundreds went,
  A little off his route.
Lee had Ben Butler closely pent;
  Grant went to let him out.

He then invested Petersburg
  With all its rebel crew,
And, soon as he had men enough,
  Invested Richmond, too.

The struggle here was long and hard,
  And lasted winter through;
It took so many men to guard
  Each rebel avenue.

The rebel works were very strong,
  And mounted well with guns.
To take these works by siege or storm
  Was anything but fun.

But when spring-time had come at last,
  And Grant was well prepared,
He forced some of the strongest works
  The enemy had reared.

And Sheridan in open fight
  Lee's cavalry had whipped;
'Tis said when Davis saw the sight,
  "He raised his voice and wept."

Lee could no longer hold the forts,
  So quickly did retreat;
Davis to the same course resorts,
  But they no more did meet.

Davis was shortly after caught
  "Way down in Tennessee,"
While Sheridan, to fury wrought,
  Hard pressed the flanks of Lee.

But Lee, retreating, bravely fought,
  And captured would not be,
Till Sheridan his way had blocked
  With dauntless cavalry.

And Grant, with equal vigor pressed
  So hard upon his rear
That terms, which gave both armies rest,
  He did consent to hear.

Their rifles, swords, and cannon, all
  Were stacked upon the ground;
All rebel soldiers within call
  To keep the peace were bound.

Brave comrades parted with regret;
  Proud Lee did sadly feel
"He had at last a foeman met
  Well worthy of his steel."

"Take back your sword," says Grant to Lee,
  "No braver can it wield;
Go with your men and horses free;
  I will your honor shield.

" Let all your swords to plowshares turn,
  Your horses plow the ground,
And, as your daily bread you earn,
  May peace and joy abound."

God bless the men who bravely fought
  Our Union to restore,
And who restored our country's flag,
  To wave from shore to shore.

And to the "bravest of the brave,"
  Grant, Sherman, Sheridan,
May grateful States accord their praise,
  Until the doom of man.

God grant we may be kind to all
  Who joined the Union camps,
All who obeyed their country's call,
  From leaders down to tramps,

And ne'er forget the men who died
  To free our land from slaves,
But every year, with grateful pride,
  Strew flowers o'er their graves.

But, above all, praise God who keeps
  Our country in his care,
And ever guides her wayward feet,
  Whether in peace or war.

And if a *leader* or a *guide*
  She needs from Heaven sent,
He ever will, as now, provide
  A LINCOLN or a GRANT.

THE MEN OF FORTY-NINE.

PART I.

WHEN gold was first discovered
  In California sand,
   There came a rush of emigrants
From almost every land.
Through each State in the Union,
  And sister Mexico,
Was heard the echo, trumpet-toned,
  For California, ho!

The noblest race that ever graced
  The human form divine
Were early Californians,
  The men of forty-nine.

They came from the British Islands
  And valley of the Rhine,
The mountain lands of Switzerland,
  And Italy's fair clime,
From the frozen plains of Russia
  And Sweden's rocky shore,
And rushed to California,
  In search of golden ore.
           The noblest race, &c.

Some sailed over the mighty deep,
  Some came across the plains,
All men of giant enterprise,
  And some with giant brains;
No matter of what country, or
  Religion, language, clime,
They all alike were welcome then
  To labor in the mines.
           The noblest race, &c.

They came to Sacramento first,
  Then scattered through the mines,
And, though they had no government,
  All were to peace inclined;
They met in every mining camp
  For to enact their laws,
And, as there were no lawyers then,
  Each pleaded his own cause.
          The no lest race, &c.

There were no thieves or robbers then,
  No need of lock and key.
The man that took another's goods
  Was hanged upon a tree.
And to decide each other's rights
  They met in council grave;
Then each would see the law enforced
  With steady hand and brave.
          The noblest race, &c.

No taxes were required then
  To tempt official pelf,
And all the gold-dust that was saved
  Was laid upon a shelf,
For every one had kindly thoughts
  Of wife or sweetheart dear,
And only thought a year or two
  For to remain out here.
          The noblest race, &c.

But, oh! how changed is everything
  Since that eventful year.
Where are the men of forty-nine,
  And those they held most dear?
Many now sleep beneath the sands
  On California's breast,
And some at home or foreign lands
  Have found eternal rest.
          The noblest race, &c.

Others still live and love to tell
  Of joys and dangers past,
Of mammoth strikes, and brave men's deeds,
  Too noble far to last.
Some, having fortunes long since made,
  To live at ease incline;
Others still labor as of yore
  In eighteen forty-nine.
          The noblest race, &c.

A young and gentler race have come,
　And spread o'er hill and dale,
And now will each one lend an ear,
　And listen to my tale.
Though rooted in the soil as firm
　As mountain oak or pine,
May God forbid they should forget
　The men of forty-nine.

The noblest race that ever graced
　The human form divine,
God bless the Californians,
　The men of forty-nine.

PART II.

From Asia's distant coast there came,
　Attracted by the mines,
A dwarfish, servile race with cues
　That reached the ground behind.
They mingled not with other men,
　Nor seemed the least refined.
In all respects, they differed from
　The men of forty-nine.

The meanest race that e'er disgraced
　The human form divine,
Were dirty, thieving Chinamen,
　Who came in forty-nine.

The men were all by nature thieves,
　Their women worse than brutes;
They had a conclave all their own
　To settle their disputes.
They classed as wild barbarians
　The men of forty-nine,
And thought to violate their laws
　Could scarcely be a crime.
　　　　The meanest race, &c.

Full thirty years this race have cursed
　This land of wheat and gold,
Our courts employed, our prisons filled
　As full as they could hold.
They have no children to support,
　And none to educate,
And all who work for the same pay
　Must share with them their fate.
　　　　The meanest race, &c.

They claim no home among our race;
  They do not come to stay,
And even those who chance to die
  Are boxed and sent away.
They have no feeling for the land
  Which they have helped to spoil,
Nor even leave their carcasses
  To fertilize the soil.
      The meanest race, &c.

Their filth the worst contagion breeds
  That mankind ever knew;
Whether in cities or on plains
  They are a filthy crew.
Their houses, if such filthy holes
  Even deserve the name,
Often through carelessness take fire,
  And set our towns in flame.
      The meanest race, &c.

China could very easy spare
  One hundred million men,
Such men as these base coolies are,
  And be the better then.
But woe to us if we receive
  One-tenth that number here.
We very soon would have to leave,
  And seek some other sphere.
      The meanest race, &c.

They would our country overrun,
  Our substance would devour,
And, by outnumbering three to one,
  Our armies overpower.
What miseries our race would see,
  When driven from their home.
Let all who think such things can't be,
  Read " Gibbons' Fall of Rome."
      The meanest race, &c.

Can we on Congressmen rely
  To stop the coolie trade?
While steamships have a subsidy
  And millions can be made,
Shall the Pacific's restless waves
  Still bear them to our coast,
And this fair land be cursed with slaves,
  While we of freedom boast?
      The meanest race, &c.

Wait yet a little longer, friends,
　　And see what may be done.
The darkest night in glory ends,
　　Chased by the rising sun.
Our slothful Government may rouse
　　And do us justice yet.
Our righteous cause it may espouse,
　　Before our sun shall set.

The meanest race that e'er disgraced
　　The human form divine,
A curse upon the Chinamen,
　　Who came in forty-nine.

————o————

TO MARY—THE MOUNTAIN GIRL.

I KNEW a girl thirteen years old,
　　Tall, yet not very slim,
Like cedars on the mountains bold,
　　So beautiful and trim.

I saw her on her way to school;
　　She had five miles to walk.
She did not wish to be a fool,
　　But learn to write and talk.

I heard her speak a piece of prose,
　　Which she had learned quite well,
From the beginning to the close.
　　She did most girls excel.

I saw her swinging to and fro
　　Up in a young pine tree.
Its top waved swiftly high and low,
　　Which quite astonished me.

I saw her next on horse-back ride;
　　She rode with graceful speed.
She had no waiter by her side,
　　Nor any did she need.

She did not have her horse led round,
　　As girls do at the bay,
But mounted quickly from the ground,
　　And swiftly rode away.

And next I saw her hauling wood
 Upon a two-horse sled.
Her dress was very plain, though good;
 A hat was on her head.

She stood erect; her whip she cracked;
 Was quickly out of sight,
But soon returned with wood *burnt black*,
 Her face as black as night.

I saw her at her cottage home;
 Her mother was away.
Her father had to dinner come,
 And wished that I would stay.

Her dinner was as nice as would
 Be got up anywhere.
Her bread was very light and good,
 And plentiful the fare.

Let dashing belles their silks unfurl,
 In cities near the sea,
But give to me the mountain girl,
 She is the girl for me.

————o————

LINES ON THE DEATH OF LITTLE MAGGIE FOOT.

SHE was a gentle, loving child,
 An angel here below;
On all her friends did sweetly smile,
 And childish love bestow.

She scarce could lisp a mother's name,
 In childish accents sweet.
We ne'er shall hear her voice again,
 Or music of her feet.

No more shall sound her charming voice
 All through the village inn;
For she is now her Saviour's choice,
 An angel, free from sin.

Parents and sisters should not mourn;
 She now is free from pain;
And what appears to be their loss,
 Is her eternal gain.

10

She is not dead,—she only slept;
  She has awoke above.
Bright angels have their vigils kept,
  Sent through a Saviour's love.

" Weep not for me," she fain would say,
  In gentle tones of love;
" I was with you but yesterday,
  To-day, with Christ above.

" Come unto me," the Saviour said,
  " Ye little ones of earth;
And let their coming none forbid;
  I claim them from their birth."

Let all mankind the lesson share
  Which Christ to man has given;
Save ye become as children are,
  Ye cannot enter Heaven.

OF all God's works 'neath heaven's span,
The noblest is an honest man.

THE fairest sight an angel sees,
A fair young girl upon her knees.

---o---

MY HUMBLE HOME.

I HAVE built me a cot in the midst of a grove.
  Three tall pines of the grove form its walls;
From the trunk of another its shingles were rove;
  Its rafters young pines straight and tall.

Not a hand save my own did its timber prepare,
  And erect in the form of a house;
Not a stick of sawed lumber or window is there;
  For a door some rough shakes come in use.

The scenery around it is awfully grand;
  In the distance vast mountains of snow,
The huge river, hills, our rapt visions command,
  While Tuolumne thunders below.

Here the owls and wild beasts serenade me by night,
  While they roam by the light of the moon;
And the boughs of the pine seem to dance with delight,
  As they hum their monotonous tune.

GREAT MANITOU,

The God of the Indian, and His Gentle Daughter, California.

I SING of pleasant foot-hills nigh,
    Of valleys, plains, and water,
Great Manitou on mountains high,
    And Cala., his fair daughter.

From high Nevada's storm-clad peaks,
    Mid clouds and drifting snows,
Great Manitou in thunder speaks.
    And shakes the world below.

His wintry storms below he hurls,
    The tempest fierce he blows;
His snow-white banner he unfurls,
    And with the storm he goes.

He keeps his secret dwelling-place
    Up in the mountains high.
No living man has seen his face;
    To see it, he must die.

His rivers rise on mountains steep,
    In everlasting snow,
And rush through rugged cañons deep,
    To reach the plains below.

These mighty rivers, wide and deep,
    Swift down their channels flow;
They dash o'er precipices steep,
    And roaring onward go.

When swelled by melting snow and rains,
    They rush in thunder down,
And overflow the grassy plains,
    O'er cottage, farm, and town.

The plains are flooded when he wills,
    The mountains clad with snow;
But in the gentle, low foot-hills
    He lets the young grass grow.

These floods do fearful losses bring
    To people on the plain,
And show that Manitou is king,
    And will his power maintain.

Their fields are covered deep with sand,
    Their cattle starved or drowned;
Their houses, when built on low land,
    Are lost and never found.

But when the land again appears,
    And grass grows everywhere,
His daughter tries, with smiles and tears,
    The damage to repair.

The moistened plains and hills and trees
    She strews with lovely flowers;
She fans them with a gentle breeze,
    And waters them with showers.

She loads the trees and vines with fruit;
    She grows vast fields of grain;
And tries her best each one to suit,
    Throughout her happy reign.

Now summer comes, and to the plains
    The streams full banks do flow.
To fill the place of absent rains,
    They come from melting snow.

The gard'ner now may try his skill
    Upon the richest ground.
He makes it rain when'er he will,
    And plenty does abound.

Great Manitou! what fields of grain
    Grow on these boundless plains;
Among the hills, what luscious fruits
    Grow ample without rains—

The peach, the apple, and the grape,
    The apricot and pear;
The orange grows through most the State,
    And figs grow everywhere.

Vast fields of gold, in former times,
    Brought thousands to these shores;
And some, charmed by the mountain clime,
    Still search for precious ores.

And some have settled on the plains,
    The golden wheat to grow;
Others high up among the pines,
    Close to the melting snow.

Plenty the work that may be done,
    And free homes everywhere,
From the vast plains with torrid sun,
    To mountains cool and rare.

Plenty rich veins of golden ore
    Among these grand foot-hills,
From the high summit to the shore,
    To run ten thousand mills.

'Tis men of means this country wan
    Men with grand cash in hand;
And when they wisely lay it out,
    Vast fortunes they command.

Yet a small secret I must tell,
    On which all can rely;
That they who wish to prosper well,
    Must see before they buy.

No RUBY that was ever found
    Outshines a noble mind.
It sheds its peerless rays around,
    And blesses human kind.

                      ANON.

AND thus the friends who hover near
    When fortune's sun is warm,
Are startled if a cloud appear,
    And fly before a storm.

                      ANON.

A LITTLE child with sparkling eyes,
    And dimples on her chin,
Has often taught me to be wise,
    And shun the path of sin.

I HAVE done, and left undone, many things which I sincerely regret having done or left undone. But it is too late to rectify the past. I have only the future now before, and that future is involved in a labyrinth of uncertainty and doubt.

SONORA.

S ONORA, the queen of the mountains,
 The "sweet home" of the fair and the brave,
Her streets are well watered with fountains,
 Where the flag of our Union doth wave.

Her beautiful homes among locusts,
 Her rich mines of bright, glittering gold,
Her fruits most delicious invoke us,
 A grand sight for the eye to behold.

Her gardens are blooming with roses,
 And fair lilies bespangled with dew,
Where the humming-bird softly reposes,
 And the bees their sweet labors pursue.

She's fan'd by the breeze of the mountains,
 Which comes charged with elixir of health,
And kisses her cool crystal fountains,
 And the cheeks of her maidens by stealth.

Her maidens are fair as the morning,
 When the lark meets the bright rising sun;
Sweet blushes their faces adorning,
 From the dawn till the evening is done.

Her sons and her daughters make music,
 Which floats on the charmed breeze of the eve,
And cheers up the heart of the stranger,
 Who a welcome is sure to receive.

My regards to the sons of Sonora,
 And my love to her daughters so fair.
I left their sweet presence in sorrow,
 Yet though banished I will not despair.

I am now in search of a treasure
 That is hidden down deep in a mine;
And writing a book at my leisure,
 Yet though sad I will never repine.

———o———

LOVE ONE ANOTHER.

T O him who wisely takes a wife
 In sweet companionship for life,
  His home a Heaven on earth will prove,
  If all his actions end in love.

As to the woman let me say,
'Tis her's to love and to obey;
And if she tries her plans to force,
'Twill end in hatred and divorce.

A man although most learned and wise,
Still with his wife he should advise,
That she may enter in his plan,—
None like a wife can help a man.

No man should even dare in strife,
To lay his hand upon his wife—
But, guided by the Powers above,
Should lead her by the power of love.

Not e'en a dog with anger blind,
Will bite the female of his kind;
And shall proud man with heavenly birth,
Outdo the meanest brute on earth?

Although most sons of Adam's race
Through anger do themselves disgrace,
The wife should, with a gentle hand
And loving words, the peace command.

And if a wife should chance to scold,
Or tantalize her husband bold,
He should not in the strife assist,
But end the quarrel with a kiss.

Each one should hide the other's fault,
Each other's virtues each exalt,
And each to each be ever true,
And oft the pledge of love renew.

So feast on love and pleasure sweet,
With home and happiness complete,
And they may live as two in one,
With Heaven's blessings on their home.
Groveland, March 3, 1879.

————o————

QUESTIONS.

————

[Respectfully dedicated to Chas. Schofield, Esq.*]

I'VE read your poem—dropped a tear.
O'er every lovely precept in it,
But through it all this thought *would* veer—
What prompted Charley to begin it?

We know a poet's range of thought
   Takes in most every theme that's charming,
But here, through every line, I've caught
   A gleam of something quite alarming!

Said I, "*I* learned the bliss that wreathes
   A married life, from Hymen's College;
Where, in the name of all that breathes,
   Did our friend Schofield get *his* knowledge?

"No dainty wife has clasped his hand,
   Or had the power to chain or hold him;
Nor has he, by a harsh command,
   Bestowed on one the power to scold him.

"How can he thus so sweetly trace
   The sentiments that bind earth's creatures,
Since all he knows of wedded grace
   He certainly has learned from teachers?

"Or else at witching hour of night,
   His tired head resting on a bowlder—
He may have dreamed (Oh, pleasure's height!)
   A wife's head leaned upon his shoulder!

"And in the day a fancy rose
   From out the wrecks of the ideal,
And thus his poem to us shows
   The rapture, when the dream is real!"

Oh, friend! advice is always good,
   And poetry, when nice, alluring;
But I do really wish you would
   Just think of all you are enduring—

To see in dreams ecstatic bliss,
   And when awake, the joy of others—
How is it you have noted this,
   And not gained profit from your brothers?

And when your words such joys reveal,
   And show your heart to be so ample,
How sad some loving girl will feel
   To know you write *without example!*
               —*Mrs. W. A. Duchow.*

*Having reference to his poem, "Love One Another."

TRUE LOVE.

[Respectfully dedicated to Mrs. W. A. Duchow.]

LOVE rules the court, the camp, the grove,
The earth beneath, and Heaven above.
Love is Heaven, and Heav'n is love."—*Scott.*

Your "Questions" have been quite too hard,
And much perplexed the mountain bard.
Suspended between hopes and fears,
He has delayed these three long years.
Procrastination, thief of time,
Should be indicted for the crime.

It is the glory of a priest
To preach on doctrines known the least;
The editor to publish news,
And on all subjects give his views.
The politician moves the crowd
To peals of laughter long and loud.
The statesman, learned in nature's laws,
Notes an effect, and seeks the cause.
The poet, in the mountains wild,
Without a home, or wife, or child,
A burden to himself would prove,
Could he not dream and write of love.

Before the world I do declare
Of love I never had my share,
Nor yet my share of kisses sweet,
Or literary food to eat;
Yet while their loss I do deplore,
I love and cherish them the more.

The man who never had a wife
Appreciates a married life,
And thinks a fair and loving bride
Would be an angel by his side,
And will make any sacrifice
To win so glorious a prize;
But when at last the prize is won,
The trouble has but just begun.

Alas! it is a common fate
For man to be intemperate;
And quite as much so, too, I think,
In love and passion as in drink.

The only case where love stands proof
Is where the lovers keep aloof,
And each from each remain exempt.
Too much caressing breeds contempt.
'Tis said brave Anthony of old
This way did Cleopatra hold.
Of love they scarcely had their fill,
And so remained true lovers still.

Love is a strange, mysterious thing.
It from the human heart does spring,
But is sometimes brought out by chance,
And holds us as if in a trance.
But love may cultivated be,
And grow like any plant or tree;
And those to whom most joy does come,
Produce and keep their love at home.

'Tis easy quite for men and wives
To grow in love through all their lives.
The one may plant the tender shoot,
The other dig about its root.
And in the dry, unfruitful years,
They both must water it with tears;
And through each long cold winter storm
Must house the plant and keep it warm;
And while its leaves are fresh and green,
No one should ever come between
To lay a hand upon a shoot,
Its sacred blossoms to pollute,
Till a gigantic tree of love
Shall reach from earth to Heaven above,
Where angels gather in the fruit,
While truth still lingers at the root.
Its trunk a road to Heaven is made,
And thousands sport beneath its shade.

True love is not an idle thing,
To temporary pleasure bring,
But is a gift of God above.
Our very being hangs on love.
It is designed by Heaven's grace
To spread and multiply our race;
And they who love each other true
Will also love their children too.

They who love's purpose missupply,
In misery must live and die.

Some do a perfect failure prove,
By taking passion for true love;
And some enough vile passion know
To send them with the d—d below.

Friend, if you know of some fair Miss,
Like me a stranger to a kiss,
With disposition kind and good,
And skill to earn her clothes and food,
One who prefers a married life,
And will consent to be my wife,
Send her to me, and we will prove
The joy and bliss of wedded love,
And to the outside world will show
What true and constant love can do;
And in our ecstasy will bless
Sonora's charming poetess.

————o————

LINES

Upon the Death of the Four Little Children of Mr. and
Mrs. Drew, of Groveland.

[Written February 16, 1879.]

ONE day in January last,
In Groveland's quiet streets I passed
  A place with pleasant shade,
Where, near a house with grassy yard,
And fence in front their home to guard,
  Three gentle children played.

Within the door the mother sat,
Her little babe upon her lap,
  And watched their childish joy.
The youngest three were lovely girls,
With sparkling eyes and dancing curls;
  The oldest was a boy—

A noble boy as could be found
Within ten miles of country round,
  A noble, manly boy.
He was a friend to all he knew,
Most truthful, upright, honest, too;
  His father's pride and joy.

The glow of health was on each cheek,
And every eye then seemed to speak
   Of happiness complete.
As through the mountain vales I roam,
I sometimes see more costly homes,
   But happier ne'er meet.

One little month this scene has changed.
It seems to all most passing strange
   Those little ones are gone,
The parents only left to weep.
Their children in the grave do sleep,
   And they are left alone.

In four small graves, ranged side by side,
Just in the order which they died,
   These four loved children lay.
Their bodies rest beneath the ground;
Their souls eternal life have found,
   By angels borne away.

And even now, though strange it seems,
We sometimes see them in our dreams,
   And join their childish play;
But when we try their hands to grasp,
Or forms unto our bosoms clasp,
   They flee from us away.

————o————

THE MOUNTAIN MAID.

WHILE passing through a mountain gorge,
   Borne by a six-horse stage,
We stopped beside a vineyard large,
   Our hot thirst to assuage.

A stream came rushing through the glade,
   And watered all below.
A cottage nestled in the shade,
   Safe from the sun's fierce glow.

Beneath a fig-tree's ample shade
   The sturdy owner sat,
And by his side a lovely maid
   Beguiled him with her chat.

"Come to the house," the father said,
   "And taste my native wine;
Although 'tis from this vineyard made,
   It equals that from Rhine."

The girl then brought a pitcher full,
  As quickly as she could,
Fresh from the cellar, nice and cool.
  We all pronounced it good.

The trees and vines were fresh and green,
  Though bowed with ripening fruit.
A lovelier place is seldom seen
  Near Pina Blanca Butte.

And as the coach away did whirl,
  Though scarce a word was said,
Each one thought of that lovely girl,
  That dark-eyed mountain maid.

. . . .

Again I passed; that girl had gone.
  She was decoyed away
From her kind father and her home,
  With *human fiends* to stay.

A man, blear-eyed, with visage rough,
  And heart as black as sin,
Had vowed to her eternal love,
  If she would go with him.

A woman who her sex disgraced,
  Who scoffed at virtue's ways,
Gave them a refuge at her place,
  And helped the foul disgrace.

These two well-mated fiends of hell
  Her ruin did effect.
No one could save her from their spell,
  Or deep damnation check.

. . . .

When next I passed, with grief severe
  The old man bowed his head,
And softly whispered, with a tear,
  " My darling child is dead."

. . . .

About three days before she died,
  While smitten with remorse,
He sought to lay his guilt aside,
  By marrying her corpse.

. . . .

At a grand ball a short time since,
  Amid the proud array
This deep-dyed villain led the dance,
  The gayest of the gay.

Is there no law to punish crime,
　Or deeds of carnage stop?
Must fashion in her flight sublime
　Bear such base villains up?

Must innocence be sunk in shame,
　And slain that shame to hide,
While her base slayer without blame
　Floats safe on fashion's tide?

Great God! how long must such things be?
　When will the young be wise?
And when will good society
　Such villainy despise?

Groveland, March 23, 1879.

————o————

SONORA, THE QUEEN OF THE MOUNTAIN.

SONORA, the queen of the mountains,
　The home of the fair and the brave,
Her streets are well watered with fountains,
　Where the flag of our Union does wave.

Her beautiful homes amid locusts,
　Her mines of bright, glittering gold,
Her fruits most delicious invoke us—
　A grand sight for the eye to behold.

Her gardens are blooming with roses,
　And lilies besprinkled with dew,
Where the humming-bird sweetly reposes,
　And the bees their sweet labors pursue.

Her sons and her daughters make music,
　Which floats on the breeze of the eve,
And enraptures the heart of the stranger,
　Who a welcome is sure to receive.

Her maidens are fair as the morning,
　When the lark meets the bright, rising sun,
Sweet blushes their faces adorning
　From the dawn till the evening is done.

Here's a health to the sons of Sonora,
　And a kiss to her daughters so fair.
Should I meet with a fortune to-morrow,
　I am sure I would spend my life there.

THE FAIREST OF THE FAIR.

I KNOW of many charming girls,
With soft blue eyes and auburn curls,
Which gently down their fair necks twirl,
  And whose cheeks bear the glow of aurora.
And some I know whose eyes are dark,
And gleam with lightning's vivid spark,
With voices sweeter than the lark,
  In the beautiful town of Sonora.

And one I know with hazel eyes,
In which true love and honor lies,
Her heart a perfect paradise;
  And her cheeks bear the glow of aurora,
Her long, dark, flowing, wavy hair,
And swan-like neck and bosom fair,
With gentle hills half hidden there,
  In the beautiful town of Sonora.

With pretty feet and slender waist,
And faultless form, my girl is graced;
Sweet blushes linger on her face,
  And her cheeks bear the glow of aurora.
When she is dressed with modest care,
None with my darling can compare.
She is the fairest of the fair
  In the beautiful town of Sonora.

————o————

VALENTINE.

[To Norah, February 14, 1881.]

SOMETIMES I write in verse for fun,
  Sometimes for fame or glory;
But of all writing that I've done,
  I'd rather write for Norah.

I own that I am twice her age,
  My beard is growing hoary;
Yet, were I wiser than a sage,
  I still must think of Norah.

Had I a pretty cottage home
  In Groveland or Sonora,
No more with strangers would I roam,
  But stay at home with Norah.

Had I a million all in gold
(I tell no idle story),
Or mines or railroad stocks unsold,
I would divide with Norah.

Were I an honored president,
Crowned with official glory
Or world-wide fame, I'd be content
To share it all with Norah.

————o————

ROYAL TOASTS.

A T a dinner given by the Lord Mayor of London, some years since, after the queen and ladies had retired, and the wines had been freely sampled and discussed, the following toasts are said to have been given:—

First toast by the Russian Minister:—

The great Russian bear: His hindfeet rest on Europe, and his forefeet on Asia, and when he growls, both continents are filled with terror and dismay.

Second, by the British Minister:—

The British lion: His lair is upon the British Isles, but the whole earth is his hunting-ground, and when he roars, all nations fear and tremble.

Third, by the American Minister:—

The great American mastodon: When he eats, boundless forests disappear from before him, and ever and anon vast mountains rise behind him. To quench his thirst, great lakes are drained to their cavernous depths, and mighty rivers spring from beneath his feet. When undisturbed, his disposition is mild and peaceful, but his anger is terrible. When in a rage he shakes the earth from pole to pole.

The other Ministers present remained silent, and the great dinner-party soon broke up, with three rousing cheers and a tiger for America.

THE WHEEL GOES ROUND.

THOUGH daily we may plan and plot,
  Each day we are sure to find,
To our distress, that things are not
  Exactly to our mind;
And useless 'tis to grieve and fret,
  Or meet our fate with frowns,
For life was never perfect yet
  Without its ups and downs.
      The wheel goes round and round;
        The wheel goes round and round;
      And those who are now at the top
        Will soon be on the ground;
      And those who at the bottom lie
        Will then be at the top;
      For so the wheel goes round and round,
        And round, and will not stop.

To-day my neighbor soareth high
  On fortune's favoring breeze;
His wants abundant streams supply;
  His life is one of ease;
His cup of pleasure and delight
  Seems sparkling to the brim;
The sun is on his path so bright
  That many envy him.
      And yet the wheel goes round;
        The wheel goes round and round;
      And those who now are at the top
        Will soon be on the ground;
      And those who at the bottom lie
        Will then be on the top;
      For so the wheel goes round and round,
        And round, and will not stop.

Some labor hard from day to day
  To till the stubborn soil,
While some from morn till evening gray
  Reap rich reward for toil;
And those who in their early youth
  Escape much grief and care,
May, when old age creeps on in truth,
  Life's heaviest burdens bear.
      The wheel goes round and round;
        The wheel goes round and round;

And those who now are at the top
 Will soon be on the ground;
And those who at the bottom lie
 Will then be at the top;
For so the wheel goes round and round,
 And round, and will not stop.
                           —*Josephine Pollard.*

————o————

WAY UP AMONG THE PINES.

WAY up among the pines
 There lives a family
To whom these rough, unvarnished lines
 Shall dedicated be.
Their complexions are red,
 From their feet to their head,
And their slanderous tongues many good people dread
 Way up among the pines.

As people pass along the road,
 I ofter hear it said,
They hear great mines of wrath explode
 On some devoted head.
The stoutest heart will fail,
 The darkest face grow pale.
The racket resembles a fish woman's wail,
 Way up among the pines.

Ye mountain men and maidens fair,
 Be careful what you do.
These vixens with the flaming hair
 May yet turn loose on you,
With their clatter-t-bang
And their Billingsgate slang,
As they often have done till the great mountains rang
 Way up among the pines.

————o————

THE OLD SUSQUEHANNA.

I STILL in memory dwell
 On the old Susquehanna,
Among scenes I loved so well,
 On the old Susquehanna.
It was in my younger days
That I learned her crooked ways,
And my skill deserved some prais
 On the old Susquehanna.

I once lived upon a branch
   Of the old Susquehanna,
Where they built rafts, good and staunch,
   On the old Susquehanna.
But the river grows more wide,
As we down her bosom glide,
And we dip our oars with pride
   On the old Susquehanna.

How I loved the stirring scenes
   On the old Susquehanna,
And likewise the pork and beans
   On the old Susquehanna.
And all nature sweetly smiled,
As we passed the lovely isles,
And we plowed the waters wild
   On the old Susquehanna.

We dashed down the great falls
   On the old Susquehanna,
And along the mighty walls
   On the old Susquehanna.
As we ran Shumakin Shute,
And likewise old Nantacoke,
Swiftly down our raft did scoot
   On the old Susquehanna.

We dashed through reefs of rocks
   On the old Susquehanna,
And we met with some hard knocks
   On the old Susquehanna.
And we ran clear through to tide,
Where the bay is large and wide,
And the tall ships seaward glide,
   On the old Susquehanna.

It was many years ago,
   On the old Susquehanna,
When a sailing I did go
   On the old Susquehanna.
But I never since have met
A more brave and jolly set;
I in fancy see them yet
   On the old Susquehanna.

OUR MARTYRED PRESIDENT.

OUR President, the nation's choice,
Elected by the public voice,
Has, by base treachery, been slain
By one who hoped a place to gain.

May public vengeance swift arise,
And plague the villain till he dies;
Then may God grant the wretch a cell
Within the inmost vaults of hell.

All who may dare to raise a hand
Against the ruler of our land,
May their accursed memory
Sink in eternal infamy.

————o——

OUR INDEPENDENCE DAY.

IN seventeen hundred seventy-six,
Proclaimed by cannon's roar,
Our Independence day was fixed
To stand forevermore.

The little ripple on our shore
Became a tidal wave,
Which, rushing onward with a roar,
Will every country lave,

Until our Goddess Liberty
Shall rule on every shore
With justice and equality,
Till time shall be no more.

————o——

OUR ANCESTORS.

OLD Adam was our great grandad,
And Eve our great grandmother;
Their oldest son one day got mad,
And killed his younger brother.

God cursed him, and he fled for life;
He feared an angry God,
But some years later took a wife
From out the land of Nod.

Mankind grew very bad indeed,
  Soon after Adam's fall,
And God resolved save Noah and seed
  He would destroy them all.

God showed Noah how to build an ark,
  And have it fitly stored;
Noah to the voice of God did hark,
  And all were safe on board.

Full forty days the sun was dark,
  And down the waters poured,
And all save those upon the ark
  By angry waves devoured.

At last the voyage was safely done,
  The ark was high on shore,
And a new race was then begun
  By each brave son of Noah.

Shem's race in Asia took their home;
  Ham peopled Africa;
The sons of Japhet, doomed to roam,
  To Europe took their way.

———

Abram met Sarah at the well,
  Where she had come for water,
And at first sight in love he fell
  With Asia's fairest daughter.

Says he: "If thou wilt be my wife
  Thou never shalt be jilted,
But I will cling to thee through life;
  Say, wilt thou?" and she wilted.

'Tis said this is a world of change; ·
  In some respects 'tis so,
But courting now was just the same
  Four thousand years ago.

From this pair sprang a mighty race,
  Who freedom's flag unfurled,
And whose deeds fill important space
  In history of the world. .

They now are scattered far and wide,
  Through every land on earth,
Wherever human kind abide,
  And still maintain their worth.

Their sons in commerce do excel;
   Their daughters, true and fair.
All love that state which pleased so well
   The great ancestral pair.

Let Ingersoll and Darwin prate
   And scoff at truths divine;
They trace their ancestry to apes—
   To Adam I trace mine.

————o————

VILLAGE SCANDAL.

IN Groveland's quiet shades there lives
   A man called Jack;
To labor little time he gives,
   But much to talk.

No matter what the subject be,
   From Adam's fall,
Through time and vast eternity,
   He knows it all.

Knows each one's private business, too,
   Or thinks he does;
Each avocation, old or new,
   Plain or abstruse.

His partner, too, a fit helpmeet,
   Adopts his views,
And daily promenades the street
   In search of news.

She learns all that's going on
   Throughout the town;
Each venture that is lost or won,
   And notes it down.

She hunts for filth in every place,
   And snuffs the scent;
To drag the pure down to disgrace,
   Her whole intent.

Sweet, helpless innocence the most
   She seeks to crush;
From good society she boasts
   Some she will thrust.

The scandal she each day collects
  By the wholesale;
To have the much desired effect,
  She must retail.

And thus by working every way
  With devotion,
She keeps the village night and day
  In commotion.

And when the injured make demand
  Facts to obtain,
She just refers them to her man
  To make all plain.

He proves by her and she by him
  The tales they've told,
And if you leave it all to them,
  'Tis good as gold.

But if for truth you further hunt,
  He quakes with fear,
And brings his partner to the front;
  He takes the rear.

————o————

ADVENTURES OF A BLUE-JAY AS RE-LATED BY HIMSELF.

AN ALLEGORY.

I TRAVELED very far and fast,
  But found a pleasant place at last,
  Where I could stop and have a rest.
This was the Mountain Eagle's Nest.

Here everything was clean and neat,
And plenty in the house to eat.
His mate presided as she should,
And every dish was nice and good.
I slept and ate and drank my fill,
Then asked the eagle for his bill.

He said to wealth he was no slave;
Another's goods he did not crave;
He would not rob me as some might,
But only charge me what was right.

I stopped a pleasant hour or two,
And then my journey did pursue,
And as I had not far to go,
Resolved to walk and take it slow.

The next place where I stopped to rest
Was known as the old Hen Hawk's Nest.
The hawk was home and seemed polite,
And bade me welcome for the night.
As I was quite fatigued from walk,
I sat and listened to his talk.

He said a day or two before
He entertained Lord Thundermore,
Escorting Lady Bumblebee
On her way to Yosemite.

None but the rich and great stop here;
The poorer sort go over there,
And without giving us a rest,
He pointed out the Buzzard's Nest.

Great Lady Snooks and Lord Titmouse
Have done the honors of my house,
And so have counts and gay countesses,
With grand outfits and gaudy dresses,
By far too numerous to mention;
To name them all I've no intention,
But thought I'd mention just a few
To show you what my house can do.

And lastly I am pleased to see
That you yourself have honored me
With all your learning and renown,
Which turns the country upside down.

He bowed and scraped and spread his tail,
And round the nest he took a sail.

I heard him through as on he went,
And silently gave my assent.
As things were looking rather rough,
I thought that I had heard enough,
But knew that I would have to stay
Until the next ensuing day,
For night had drawn her curtain down
O'er hills and woods and fields and town,
And being lame and tired, too,
I early to my room did go;
But as I did not feel quite right,
I did not sleep a wink that night.

I soon learned there was something wrong.
I knew the Hoot-owl by his song;
I heard the Night Hawk come and go,
The Fish Hawk and the Vulture, too.

As there I lay upon my bed,
I plainly heard what each one said;
I learned they were on plunder bent;
To rob me was their dire intent.

I could not make successful fight
Against such odds at dead of night;
To flee I knew it was too late,
So had to stay and bide my fate.

They did not give me long to wait,
But rudely dragged me through the gate;
Tore from my back my coat of blue,
And took my cap and feathers, too.
They basely stripped me naked quite,
Then cast me forth into the night,
And all that night so cold and damp,
They shouted robber, thief, and tramp.
And none dared even come that way,
Where on the cold, damp ground I lay,
Or even listen to my cry,
But left me in the cold to die.

While thus upon the ground I lay,
I fondly wished for coming day,
That I might cast a look around
To see if shelter could be found.
I thought it very hard to die
Without a friend or comrade nigh,
Yet, as I shivered in the breeze,
I surely thought that I would freeze.

But as I tried to move about,
Without a knowledge of my route,
Or scarce a consciousness of life,
Almost beyond all mortal strife,
Though yet with fear and pain oppressed,
I crawled into the Buzzard's Nest.

Old Buzzard knew me very well,
And to his mate did softly tell:
" I think we better let him lie,
As I am certain he will die,
And that will prove our benefit,
As on his body we will sit,

And then before it is too late,
Administer on his estate,
And make a thousand or two more,
The same as we have done before.

"And now don't say a single word,
And I will tell you what I've heard.
'Tis said way up among the pines
He is the owner of rich mines.

"Now if we manage right at all,
These mines into *our* hands will fall.
Should any stranger come to town
To see these mines we'll cry them down,
And if to buy is his intent,
We'll say they are not worth a cent;
And then if buy them still he would,
We'll swear the title is not good,
And thus we'll watch from day to day
To keep all mining sharps away,
Until we have these mines and lands
With a good title in our hands;
And then we'll open up the ground,
And gold in plenty will be found;
And as we yet are in our prime,
Now won't we have a splendid time?

"And now I think I better go
And find our bosom friend, the Crow,
And further still my flight pursue,
'Till I have seen the Vulture, too;
And then to make our plans complete,
If other friends I chance to meet,
I will invite them one and all
To a grand feast at Buzzard's Hall.

"We must not let the Blue-jay know
A thing that we intend to do,
And though he pays me in advance,
I'll charge him with the whole expense,
For when he's dead no one can know,
Nor can they prove a thing we do,
And all his wealth in stocks and lands
Will fall into our willing hands.

"And if his friends should raise a cry,
We all will meet them with a lie,
For I have found from early youth
A lie goes farther than the truth,

And this is just the reason why
I nearly always choose to lie,
And even when, be it confessed,
The truth would answer for the best."

He did not favor Hawks the least,
And would not have them at his feast;
And Hawks would not with Buzzards eat;
They like their food more nice and sweet,
And then the Buzzard tells his friends
That Hawks are quite too fond of Hens.
So it is very plain to see
That they agree to disagree,
And, measured by each other's rules,
The Hawks are knaves, the Buzzards fools.

They met and were as strange a crew
As any one could wish to view.
While some were of a motley white,
Some were as black as darkest night,
And all the shades of black and blue
Were found among the Buzzard's crew.

While some were dressed with decent care,
Others quite little had to wear;
Some strutted proudly as they walked,
While others bowed and laughed and talked.
Old Buzzard strutted through the hall,
And made them think he knew it all.

Just like a nest of unclean birds
They listened to his honied words,
And then, with mouths extended wide,
And eyes close shut, for more they cried;
And though he fed them stinking meat,
They gulped it down and thought it sweet.

He quite minutely told them o'er
All he had told his mate before,
And then asked what he better do;
They all resolved to help him through,
And promised not to say a word,
Or even see the hated bird.
They would no aid or comfort give,
And fondly hoped he would not live.

Three fearful weeks there I did lie,
Writhing in mortal agony;

Without a friend to make my bed,
Or smooth a pillow for my head,
And none in all the country round
Were at my bedside ever found.

None did I say? save only one,
And he was not a Buzzard's son.
It must have been by some strange chance;
He may have come there in a trance.
'Tis very strange, but is no jest,
An Eagle sought the Buzzard's Nest;
Sometimes by night and oft by day
He comforted the poor sick Jay.

I could not rest or eat or sleep,
Or stand one moment on my feet,
Or even turn myself in bed,
But lay as one already dead.

Old Buzzard daily brought me meat,
Such as a healthy man might eat,
And set it down quite near my head,
Just as the Chinese feed their dead.

But Heaven decreed I should not die,
Or longer on a sick bed lie.
My pain first ceased; then I could eat;
At last I stood upon my feet.
And all the fiends of earth or hell
Could not prevent my getting well.

Old Buzzard found his plans were balked,
And to his lovely mate he talked.
He stamped and raved and cursed and swore,
And she her raven ringlets tore.

Says she, " He is a common tramp;
I will not wait on the old scamp."

He swore he would not sleep or eat
Till I was turned into the street.

Still weak and feeble, lame and sore,
Thus I was driven from their door.
They then threw out my scanty goods,
With which I sought the friendly woods,
To seek the company of bears
And panthers, sleeping in their lairs.

The bears are generous and brave,
And only fight their lives to save;
They don't surprise a sleeping foe,
And take his life and eat him too;
Nor do they often give offense,
But only fight in self-defense;
Yet this is true, now take my word,
That when they do fight they fight hard;
They stand erect, confront the foe,
And lay him prostrate with a blow,
And then to punish him the more,
They scratch and bite and wound him sore.
I know my style of life is rough;
Full well I know 'tis bad enough,
But this I choose to shun a worse,
And thus evade a common curse.

I am no coward, braver far
Than some who snuff the smoke of war,
But choose to shun all social cares,
And brave my fortune with the bears;
For in society I find
The hawks and buzzards of mankind.
If rich, they rob us if they dare;
If poor, their insults we must bear.
They thief and tramp and robber cry,
And turn us out-of-doors to die.

Yet, trusting in the power of truth,
Which I have loved from early youth,
And hoping all will yet be right,
Kind friends, I bid you all good-night.

And as I wait the coming day,
Subscribe myself your own
Blue Jay.

———o———

OUR COUNTRY. .

WHEN tyrants drove to bloody war
  Our brave and manly sires,
And sent their forces from afar
  To desecrate our fires,

Great Washington in thunder rose,
  And, with a dauntless band,
Rolled back the war-cloud on his foes,
  And drove them from our land.

The young republic of the West,
　The child of fearful strife,
Was taken from its mother's breast,
　And nurtured into life.

Old mother England tried once more
　To force her offspring home,
And sent her war ships to our shore;
　Her troops by thousands came.

The youthful giant showed his strength,
　And, after years of war,
The foe was driven back at length,
　And dare return no more.

When fierce Rebellion reared his head
　Our Union to divide,
And Liberty was almost dead,
　And Peace her face did hide,

The great republic of the West
　Sent forth a million men,
Who did the rebel hordes invest,
　And chained them in their den.

Now let all nations know the truth,
　And fully understand,
This giant is no more a youth,
　But now a full-grown man,

A giant of no common growth;
　He loves sweet liberty,
And, mindful of his early youth,
　He hates base tyranny.

He welcomes to our peaceful shores
　The poor and the oppressed;
All such as flee from kingly powers
　May here find quiet rest.

But if an enemy oppose,
　He can a warrior be,
And hurl destruction on his foes;
　He strikes for liberty.

THE EAGLE AND THE BUZZARD.

FROM the towering crag of a mountain high,
    A brave and warlike eagle soared,
And over the flocks in a valley close by,
    His strong, swift wings were daily heard.

A buzzard sat lazily turning his head
    On one of the loftiest trees,
Snuffing for the scent of some poor creature dead,
    Which he hoped he might trace by the breeze.

The eagle paused like a knight with lance in rest,
    And then swooped swiftly down,
And bore a fine fat lamb away to his nest,
    As a feast for his brood half grown.

The old buzzard witnessed the bold eagle's plan,
    And took not a moment to wait,
But tangled his claws in the fleece of a ram,
    And then plaintively mourned his sad fate.

The moral of this ancient fable remains,
    And that I will quickly define;
The buzzard the man without money or brains,
    Who thinks he can run a quartz mine.

He can wriggle and twist however he may,
    And brace himself up with conceit,
And carry his head very high for a day;
    In the end he is surely beat.

The eagle the man who with judgment and skill
    Develops a mine that will pay,
And has plenty of cash to be drawn at will,
    Let the settlements come when they may.

He uses his means with economy, too,
    And does his own business attend;
He may make some trifling mistakes, it is true,
    But will certainly win in the end.

EDUCATION AND LIBERTY.

MAY education ever be
The bosom friend of liberty,
And may they visit hand in hand
Each town and hamlet of our land.

And may each school and college be
A bomb-proof fortress of the free;
We can but have a good report,
Where education holds the fort.

A man by education blest
Cannnot be duped by king or priest,
And a great nation of such men
On their resources may depend.

I now am poor, yet by my son
The highest honors may be won,
He may be to our Congress sent,
Or even be our President.

Or if a sword he choose to wield,
He may win honors in the field,
And from a private or a page,
Become the hero of the age.

God bless the teachers; let them come,
And thus illumine every home.
There is no need of dolts and fools,
While our free land is blest with schools.

Not far ahead I think I see
Each State with education free,
And every child induced to go,
And every useful science know.

And learn to labor, too, as well
As to keep books and buy and sell,
And thus quite independent be,
While working out their destiny.

May education ever be
The bosom friend of liberty.
And may they visit hand in hand
Each town and hamlet of our land.

And may each school and college be
A bomb-proof fortress of the free.
We can but have a good report
Where education holds the fort.

WRITTEN FOR MISS LEVETTA SCO-FIELD IN HER ALBUM.

LEVETTA, thou art Nature's child,
The fairest flower of Idlewild;
With large dark eyes and form divine,
May happiness be ever thine.

FOR MISS MINNIE S——.

The rose blooms in the mountain glen,
  The fawn goes skipping through the lea,
And shuns the company of men;
  They ever bloom and skip like thee.

FOR MISS EVA S——.

Eva is well endowed with sense,
With quiet, deep intelligence,
Designed by the great powers above
To win in learning and in love.

FOR BIRDIE S——.

Sweet Birdie, darling little pet,
A modest little violet;
Her form so fair, her heart so warm,
May angels keep my love from harm.

———o———

MY OLD CAT.

I ONCE had an old cat
That was lazy and fat,
  And she had a very long tail;
But the lazy old thing
Loved to lie still and sing,
  Or else move about like a snail.

And although rats and mice
Were quite plenty and nice,
  She never would catch one to eat.
And although most all cats
Much prefer mice and rats,
  This one much preferred other meat.

Now my friend Mr. James,
Though I'll not mention names,
   Had a dog that was glossy and black.
When this dog came around,
With a skip and a bound,
   The cat always got up her back.

On one very fine day
She went over the way
   To visit my neighbor alone.
There she found the black dog
Lying still as a log,
   Quite contentedly gnawing a bone.

The old cat gave a squall
And a leap for the wall,
   But while she was under full sail,
The dog gave a quick bound
Very high from the ground,
   And instantly snapped off her tail.

My friends made some pretense
That, to curtail expense,
   I commenced by cur-tailing my cat.
The dog's mis-anthropy
Caused the cat-astrophe;
   It was done before you could say "*scat.*"

————o————

WRITING WITHOUT PAY.

I HAVE remarked, and here repeat,
   To write for papers without pay,
Or run for office, and get beat
   Is anything but fun for me.

THOUGHTS AND CONCLUSIONS

ON READING NARRATIVES OF THE SURVIVORS OF THE JEANNETTE.

FROM all the information I have been able to glean from these narratives, and from the adventures of numerous Arctic explorers, I cannot see any insurmountable difficulty in the way of reaching the North Pole. But I am fully convinced that it will never be done through the agency of the hide-and-seek policy, which has hitherto been so unsuccessfully pursued.

A ship is fitted out and furnished in good style by some Government or individual, and started for the North Pole. This vessel forces its way as far as possible during summer, into the perpetual ice floes of the frozen North, and, as a matter of course, is frozen in during the ensuing winter, and usually remains there one, two or three years, or until it is smashed by the ice and sunk.

During all this time there is an intense interest in regard to the fate of the ship and crew, and numerous other vessels are sent out by the different nations interested, to search for them. Some of these adventurous searching vessels are in turn caught in the ice, which makes it very necessary that other vessels should be sent in search of them, and so on through the catalogue. In this way many valuable lives are lost, and much property uselessly destroyed, and but very little or nothing accomplished towards reaching the Pole.

The North Pole can be reached to a certainty, and that without any very great risk or expenditure of life or property. And it may be done by some private individual or company, or by Government, in the following manner:—

The Arctic Ocean having already been sufficiently explored to show that it is full of shoals and islands, let some suitable point of land or island be selected, as far north as it is possible and safe for vessels to visit each year with certainty, and where a chain of islands is most likely to extend northward, and there establish a good and substantial depot of all needed supplies, sufficient to last two or three years at least, and there also erect good and substantial warehouses, and warm quarters suitable for the accommodation of at least one hundred men.

The larger portion of these men should be constantly employed in exploring the sea and land still farther north, and moving supplies by the use of boats in summer when the sea is open, and by dog-sledge in winter; and branch depots or stations should be built at reasonable distances farther north, wherever suitable land can be found, until the Pole is reached.

Good roads can be built on the ice in winter, from one of these stations to another, and temporary huts, or way-stations, can be built all along the route every ten miles if necessary to insure the safety and comfort of travelers and teamsters. These cabins can be built mostly of ice. All the timber that would be necessary would be a few joice, and perhaps planks, to hold up the roof of ice. The roof and walls can be made perfectly tight by putting on water and letting it freeze.

In this manner the explorers can gradually and surely work their way north until they reach the Pole. The last two or three hundred miles nearest the Pole will no doubt be found to be comparatively smooth, unbroken ice. That in all probability is what Dr. Kane saw, instead of an open sea. If such should prove to be the case, there would be very little difficulty in making the exploration after reaching that point, as road building would no longer be necessary, and stations erected on the ice would last for years. The explorers could scan the more northern sea on skates, and hunt the seal, the walrus, and the great northern bear, around the Pole, and thus increase their supplies of food and clothing.

If this exploration should be undertaken and prosecuted with vigor, and in a proper manner, it will not take many years, or many millions of dollars, to accomplish it, and the routes may afterwards be continually kept open, so that the average tourist will not consider his travels complete until he has done the North Pole. And the lucky and adventurous company or nation which should first make the discovery, may incorporate the territory into a grand skating rink, and erect a crystal palace of ice directly on the Pole, for the accommodation of guests of all nations, and which may be illuminated during the long winter nights by the Great Northern Electric Light Company, presided over by the gorgeous Aurora herself, clothed in all her peerless, refulgent and pristine grandeur and glory.

FUNERAL ADDRESS

Of Neumasha, or Captain Lewis, the Great Chief
of the Mariposa and Tuolumne Indians
at Big Creek, Tuolumne County,
April 15, 1882.

AGAIN the voice of mourning is heard in our camps.
The mighty hills send back an answering echo to
our funeral cry.   Big Bill, the last great hunter of
our once powerful tribe, and she who proudly followed
his daring footsteps through the mountain forests
in pursuit of the fleet-footed deer, the treacherous
panther, and the savage bear, both have crossed
the dark river to the happy hunting-grounds of our
race.   She went before him to prepare his camp, and
be ready to welcome him to the select company of
the mighty hunters who have gone before, who live
forever in perpetual youth, amid abundant game, in
boundless forests beyond the reach of the white man.

Thus one after another, in quick succession, we
pass to that other shore.   I can well remember when
our daring hunters were as numerous as the trees on
yonder hills, and their glad shouts could everywhere
be heard as they surrounded the nimble deer with
belts of fire, and supplied themselves, and their wives
and little ones, with abundant meat and clothing.
The tall pine and broad-spreading oak yielded a
bountiful supply of bread; the rich soil in the mountain valleys and along the streams produced an
abundance of excellent roots, and our rivers were
full of the most delicious salmon.

But, like the trees of our forests, we have been cut
down and destroyed.   Our hunters, together with

most of our brave sons and fairest daughters, have left us, and we alone remain to mourn their untimely loss. Each succeeding year our numbers diminish and grow less, and soon there will be none left to mourn our loss, or longer tell the tale of our woes. Our villages and the last resting-places of our dead will soon be leveled by the plow, and nothing will be left on earth to show that we have ever lived.

The white man has taken possession of our lands, destroyed our game, cut down our forests, and built his homes upon our fairest hunting-grounds. The fruitful soil where the choicest roots were found has been dug up, and washed away, in search of gold. Our rivers are obstructed with dams which prevent the coming of the salmon, and our spears have long since been laid aside and forgotten.

Thus have our means of living, and the sustenance of our wives and children, one after another, been taken away from us, or destroyed, our homes desecrated, and our wives and daughters outraged. Maddened with jealous rage and oppressed with hunger, we sought to drive the invader from our homes, but he was too strong for us, and many of our bravest warriors fell, pierced by the leaden bullets from the unerring rifle in the hands of the foe. Your former great chief, Lutorio, fell, bravely fighting for his people and their rights.

At last, being overpowered and disheartened, we fled to the deep, dark recesses of the mountains, to hide ourselves from the merciless and unrelenting foe, the destroyer of our race; but he followed us even into the almost inaccessible depths of the Yosemite and Hech-Hechy. Again we sought for peace, and these many years we have freely given ourselves up to the will and pleasure of the white man; but peace has been even more destructive to us than war.

The white man has furnished us with strong

drinks which have maddened our brains, and kindled within our breasts the flames of the evil world, causing us to destroy each other. He has seduced and debauched our wives and daughters, and alienated their affections from us, their natural protectors, and they and their children have been inoculated with the most loathsome diseases known to human kind, which have made life a burden and a curse, and hurried them on to premature and untimely graves.

Very few of us have escaped this greatest and most deadly curse. And what few children there are, still living among us, have the corrupted blood of the accursed white man coursing through their veins. Their white fathers do not care for them, and their Indian mothers have mostly died and left them in the care of those of us who still live, which is a heavy burden upon us, and adds greatly to our distress. But we are fast passing away and must soon leave those children who survive us to the tender mercies of their inhuman fathers.

The white man is still upon our track, and is pressing closer and closer upon us on every side. He is ready to take the last poor remnant of land upon which our villages and burying-places are situated. He is now cutting and selling the last of our wood convenient for us, and has turned away from our gardens, and appropriated to his own use, the waters of the streams. He seems determined that nothing shall be left us to make life desirable, or even possible. And why should we linger here to constantly brood over our wrongs, and gradually, but surely, sink deeper and deeper into the soft and yielding mire of black despair?

I have long stood among you, breasting the storms of life, like a tall cedar on the mountain-top, but my head has become white with the snows of many winters, and my back is bowed beneath its heavy

weight of sorrow. Our friends and children have
nearly all crossed the dark river, and beckon us to
meet them on the other side. I can remain with you
but little longer, and feel that I shall be the last
great chieftain of our tribe. There is no one who
cares to take my place. None left to guard the interests, or advocate the rights of the last remnant of
a once powerful tribe of the despised and persecuted
race of red men. May the Great Manitou (the God
of the Indian) guard and protect each and all of you
who shall remain to mourn for me when I shall be
gathered to the home of my fathers, and my voice
shall be heard on earth no more.

[Written upon the life and supposed death of John Paul Jones, who was
supposed to have taken poison and jumped from the railroad bridge into the
river at Sacramento.]

BY HIS FRIEND.

HE was a friend as kind and true
    As one could wish to have;
Honest and industrious, too,
    Intelligent and brave.

He was a soldier through the war,
    And marched with Sherman's host,
And fought the rebels everywhere,
    In land, and on the coast.

At Chattanooga, fierce they charged
    Upon the rebel lines;
At Kenesaw they routed them,
    High up among the pines.

At Buzzard's Roost they stormed the heights,
    Nor feared the rebel yell;
To charge the foe was their delight,
    Through storms as fierce as hell.

My friend was struck with rebel lead,
    And left upon the plain;
But although he was left for dead,
    He lived to fight again.

And when they did Atlanta reach,
  The rebels held the fort;
Though hard they tried their works to breach,
  They found no idle sport,

Until brave Sherman made a plan
  To draw the rebels out,
Which was far more than they could stand,
  And ended in a rout.

Then from Atlanta to the sea
  Great Sherman led his host;
His army, in divisions three,
  All safely reached the coast.

They then marched up along the coast,
  Through South Car'lina State,
And sealed, with very little cost,
  Proud Charleston's hapless fate.

Columbia was an easy prey
  As soldiers could desire,
Though Hampton bravely stood at bay,
  And set the town on fire.

But why should I prolong my chant?
  Strong Richmond fell at last,
And Lee surrendered all to Grant;
  Peace followed war's fierce blast.

Our soldiers were released, once more
  To seek their homes in peace,
Or visit a more distant shore,
  Their fortunes to increase.

My friend to California came;
  He had the best of trade,
Though blacksmithing is rather tame,
  Compared with rebel raids.

At Groveland's classic shades he stopped,
  And said he came to stay;
Had plenty business at his shop,
  No need to go away.

He seemed in business to excel,
  And married a young wife;
His friends all thought him doing well,
  Just in the prime of life.

But business did a call engage,
  At Sacramento City,
He left a letter on the bridge,
  And here must end my ditty.

  .   .   .   .

Tell me, ye fishes of the deep,
  To me some message send!
Ye crabs, that on the bottom creep,
  Have ye beheld my friend?

  .   .   .   .

Now, two years later, comes the news
  Our hero did not die;
To take the plunge he did refuse,
  But to the mountains fly.

His wife, with whom he thus did part,
  Who loved him far too well,
Soon perished with a broken heart,
  Within a hospital.

And now, 'tis said, *he* has a home
  In Stockton's crazy house;
To a sad end they both have come.
  What fortune could be worse?

THE REPUBLICAN PARTY.

How and by Whom It Was First Organized in California. .

ETWEEN the years 1849 and 1856, I followed the business of ranching in Sacramento County, near the El Dorado County line, and, it being only a few hours' ride from my ranch to Sacramento City, business or pleasure often called me to the State capital.

Among my most intimate friends and associates at that time in Sacramento, was a gentleman in whose company I had crossed the plains in coming to California, and who was then engaged in the practice of law, and, as may well be imagined, I seldom visited the town without making a call at his office.

It was at one of these visits that my friend asked me if I would not like to take a hand in organizing a new political party. We had both belonged to a branch of the Democratic party known at that time, in the State of New York, as Bombumers; but as that was merely a local organization, and did not reach as far as California, and as we did not feel like going back into the ranks of the old "hunkers," as the old Democratic party was then called, our thoughts very naturally led us in search of some new political organization which would better satisfy a more improved and enlightened understanding. A convention had already been held at Pittsburg, Pa., under the auspices of Francis P. Blair, Sr., which had adopted a platform that was then before us, the principles of which we sincerely and heartily approved.

Under these considerations I readily consented to join the little forlorn hope, which was to meet the next evening in a small room at the old Academy of Music Building on K Street, and we were just seven in number, all told, as folllows: Leland Stanford, merchant; Charles Crocker, merchant; Huntington and Hopkins, merchants; E. B. Crocker, lawyer; Cornelius Cole, lawyer, and Charles Schofield, rancher.

We had no organized meeting, but simply an informal discussion of the new political movement in the East, and its chances of success, and how the organization could best be started in California.

Among other conclusions it was unanimously determined that it would be necessary to publish a newspaper in the interests of the new party, at Sacramento, and a stock company was then and there formed for that purpose, and all present subscribed $100 each to give it a start. And it was further determined that the new paper should be known as the *Times*, and that Cole should act as general manager and James McClatchy as editor. And then, after a somewhat lengthy and desultory discussion about other means of founding the new movement, and who would be most likely to join it, it was finally determined that each person present should act as a committee of one to see such persons as he would be likely to have the most influence with, and do all that lay in his power to forward the cause. With this understanding the meeting adjourned.

Thus was the organization of the Republican party launched in this State, but it took a long and most determined effort to put its machinery in successful working order. Among the earliest advocates of the cause, Bates had the platform upon which he was speaking torn from beneath his feet. Tracy was often hooted down, and Cole and Crocker were often refused a hearing. It was then that Colonel Baker, having espoused the cause, loomed up, like Mt. Shasta, above the turbulent waters of Democracy and No-nothingism and awed them to silence with irresistible eloquence.

But the cause eventually triumphed. Lincoln was elected and the war came. General Baker fell at the head of his brigade, with his face to the foe, bravely fighting in defense of those great principles he had advocated with such matchless eloquence, his prolific brain riddled with rebel lead. He went down beneath the great tidal wave of rebellion, "with colors flying, and all sail set." I saw his remains carefully deposited upon the summit of Lone Mountain, near the last resting-place of the lamented Broderic.

But let us now, in the beginning of the year 1886, briefly review the fortunes of the original seven organizers of the great Republican party in this State.

The first five named, after procuring substantial aid from the Government, entered heartily into the construction of the Central Pacific Railroad, which was finally pushed to its completion and made them all millionaires. E. B. Crocker and Mark Hopkins have since died. Cornelius Cole has served one term in the lower house of Congress, and one term in the Senate, and is now practicing law in the United States Courts in San Francisco.

Leland Stanford, Charles Crocker, and C. P. Hunting now hold a position among the greatest railroad magnates of the nation and the world, and not only count their fortunes by millions and tens of millions, but they are still adding millions to their fortunes each year, until they are fast becoming more powerful even than the Government itself, which first lent its aid to give them a start in the world.

But what of the seventh man, you ask? He raised a company of volunteers, modestly declined a captain's commission, and served faithfully during the war as a private soldier, and is now living, or rather staying, away back among the mountains of Tuolumne County, California, in a small log cabin, and there is none so poor as to do him reverence.

———

SOME years since, while stopping at a small village on the line of the Yosemite travel, where the stage usually stopped to change horses and give the passengers time for dinner, I one day noticed among the passengers two young English bloods who seemed to take delight in making sport of everything American.

Among other things, directly after dinner, while they were standing on the veranda of the hotel, waiting for the stage, one of them happened to notice a printed proclamation from the governor of the State, which was pasted upon the wall, calling for the usual election of the various State and county officers. He called the attention of his comrade to the poster, and, after looking it over together, one of them turned to me, saying, "You uns have queer ways of doing things in this country!" "Yes," says I, "this is a new country; you see we are still in the woods here, but when we get older we will probably get some old woman to govern us, the same as you have in England." "I wish," said he, "that blarsted stage would hurry up, and take us hout of this bloody 'ole."

THE SUNDAY LAW.

ON a bright Sunday morning in June, as I was standing near the main entrance of a saloon in a small country village, listening to the vulgar and obscene language and boisterous laughter of a party of men inside, who were engaged in playing cards for the drinks, my attention was attracted by the appearance of a very interesting and neatly-dressed young woman who approached the door, with a young child in her arms, and leading another beautiful child, a little girl of two or three summers, who was also very cleanly and prettily dressed.

On approaching the door, she very modestly and with a faltering voice requested the little girl to go into the saloon and get her father, who proved to be one of the card players at the card table. I saw her climb upon her father's chair, and putting her plump little arm lovingly around his neck, she requested him, in the sweet, innocent language of childhood, to come and take a walk with her and mamma, who was waiting for him at the door.

He took the child in his arms, and, going to the door, where his beautiful young wife was standing, he put the child down by her side, and gruffly bade her "Go home with the children; this is no place for you." I saw a large tear glisten in her soft blue eye, as she took the little girl again by the hand and turned to go. And, as she left, I almost involuntarily repeated to him his last words to his aggrieved and disappointed young wife, "GO HOME WITH THE CHILDREN; THIS IS NO PLACE FOR YOU."

But wife, home, and children had no longer any charms for him. He returned to the card table to spend the day and his last week's earnings in vile dissipation and boisterous mirth.

OUR GIRLS.

GIRLS should not expect their future husbands to support them in idleness and luxurious ease, and should therefore prepare themselves to act some useful part in the great drama of life. They cannot all marry rich men, even were it desirable, and in any case it is far better that women, as well as men, should have some useful and congenial avocation. Her daily employment should be such as will make her and those about her more contented and happy, and her home the most agreeable and desirable place on earth for her husband and children, and thus prevent them from wandering away in search of forbidden pleasures. She should chain them to her home with the silken cords of love.

But no man should make a slave of his wife, any more than she should make a slave of her husband, but each should labor for the comfort and happiness of the other, and of those precious little pledges of love which may be placed in their charge.